JACK IN THE DUST
A Jack of All Trades novel

DH Smith

Earlham Books

Published 2019 by Earlham Books
Book design & cover art by Lia at Free Your Words
(*www.FreeYourWords.com*)

Text copyright © 2019 DH Smith

ISBN: 978-1-909804-38-8

Chapter 1

The glass was shattered, its frame blackened. The fragments had been swept into a heap at one side of the door. Inside was semi darkness, Jack could make out two figures by the black walls and hear them banging. He wiped a finger against the window frame; it came off sooty.

He took a step back and screwed up his nose at the prospect of a dirty job. Before him was a three storey block of flats, fire damaged but limited to the vestibule. Once before he'd worked on a fire aftermath, and each day he'd ended up croaky and filthy. He wasn't keen to do another. Nor did he like working under a boss, but he had bills to pay and no other work on the books.

Face the man.

Should he bring his tools? He looked back to his van, just visible at the roadside. Look competent. But he wasn't sure what was needed. He'd already picked up a safety helmet, a face mask was in the pocket of his navy, paint-stained overalls. He'd be filthy in no time. There was always the choice; he could just walk away.

Get a grip. This is not forever.

Jack pushed open the wide door, much of the glass out in the small panes, sharp splinters hanging in the sides. His hand made a print on the frame, like a stone age cave impression. He blinked in the gloom, the electrics had obviously gone.

Inside were two men, faces blackened like old time minstrels, both in helmets and smudged masks. The air was thick, dusty with the stench of burnt wood. The two men

1

stopped as Jack entered. One man was middle aged, short and thick set, in overalls, the other young, wearing a torn T-shirt and jeans. The shorter man indicated outside with a gloved hand. Jack exited and the two men followed.

Outside the stocky man lowered the face mask, revealing an oval of cleanliness round his mouth, chin and half of his nose. His tongue and gums were startlingly pink in their wetness.

'You Jack Bell?' he said sharply, removing one glove and taking a phone from his pocket.

Jack nodded. 'Sorry I'm late. Got the address wrong.' He hadn't, but 'slept in' was a teenage alibi.

The man stabbed the face of his phone. 'We start at eight prompt.'

'Won't happen again.' What else could he say? New boss. Forty minutes late. It was why he preferred working alone. No one to have a go at him. Apart from customers.

The man was staring, streaking his brow with his fingers, the lines on his forehead dotted with black particles.

'I'll work the tea break,' said Jack.

'You won't,' said the man. 'But you'll be here tomorrow on time.' And half smiled as he put out his hand. 'Ben Wilson.'

Jack shook his hand.

'And this is my son, Tony.'

Tony had joined them and was making a roll-up. 'Hello, Jack.'

'Pleased to meet you.' Jack shook his hand. 'What's happened here?' he added, indicating the scarred entrance and the inside.

'Fire in the hallway and lower stairs.' Ben indicated the staircase which was half gone. 'Kids they reckon started it late in the night, stoned out their heads. Furniture dumped in the hallway caught light, then the stairs caught...' He shrugged. 'Not intentional, they reckon, but who can say?'

'Anyone hurt?'

Ben shook his head. 'No one. The fire brigade were here sharp. Got an anonymous call. They think it was from one of the youngsters. Anyway, they managed to keep the damage to the hallway, bottom stairs and front door. Our job is to clear the debris, put in a new staircase to the first floor, renew the front door and decorate. I've got you down for a week. That right?'

'It's what Bob told me.'

'I figured if Bob recommended you, you must be OK. Where's your tools?'

'There. In the van.' He pointed it out by the side of the road, Jack of All Trades painted on the side. Jack waited for the comment.

It didn't come.

'You'll need a cold chisel, club hammer, bow saw. We got to demolish before we can do any renewal.'

'How do the residents get in and out?'

'Back fire-escape. They come through the hallway, so we have to stop work when they go by. Get your tools.'

Ben turned away, pulled open the door and went back inside. His son winked, stubbed out his fag with his boot, and followed his father. Jack went to his van. Introductions done with, he had to get working.

Half an hour later, he was as dirty as his co-workers.

The walls of the hallway were scorched and cracked like a dark cavern. All the plaster would have to come off. The two flats on the ground floor had their doors scorched and would need replacing, but they'd held the fire off from the occupants. An electrician was due in a few days to fix the burnt out lighting.

The stairs were charred and badly damaged: wooden remnants between twisted metal banisters with curling black paint. A cupboard under the stairs had its door and frame half gone, the blackened plaster inside crumbling over the metal leftovers of mops and brooms whose handles and tufts were piles of ash. Between the ash, plastic pools were on the floor, like drying jellyfish, which had once been containers of cleaning products.

The three workers hammered, sawed and pulled at wood and metal. Jack was togged up in gloves, helmet, mask and goggles, his throat parched, needing frequent lubrication. A two gallon plastic bottle of water was outside the door with three metal cups. Each time he went out for a drink, into the fresh air, Jack was tempted not to go back inside. Just a couple of days, he would tell himself, to get the demolition done. Then it'd be OK. Just a couple of days of dust. Keep saying: I need the money, work is work.

A skip was due in the afternoon; the aim of the morning was to get clear the remnants of staircase and cupboard under it. Not that that would be the end of demolition. The plaster on the walls and ceiling was too blackened and damaged to stay. All of it would have to go. More dust and hazard. He'd never make a demolition worker, too aware of the tiny particles that evaded the skimpy mask.

Too much thinking time in the grainy haze. Tea break in an hour. Aim for that. Thinking too far ahead made it misery work. Just labour on, break to break, until the day is done. Two days' hard graft, all three on it, would get the demolition done. Restitution could begin in a couple of days.

Ben was up a ladder sawing the decrepit banisters, Tony in the cupboard, knocking it down around him, throwing out the detritus. Jack was working on what was left of the wooden stairs, smashing off the charred pieces, sawing where needs be. He was thinking about the work ahead, as he always did when he worked for himself. Once the fire damaged stuff was out, they'd have to remove the front door and side windows in order to get a new staircase in. Bob had said it was a week's work. Never a week. Jack could see at least a month for the three of them. The week, he guessed, was a trial, offer no more until the new bloke proved himself.

Well, having got through the worst of it, today and tomorrow, he'd make sure he was kept on for the rest of it. A month's work, if he got on well with Ben. He would. No more lateness. Think of the money, the demolition wouldn't last forever, no matter what it felt like now.

Jack was grateful when his ex, Alison, phoned. He strode outside into the warm summer air, taking a drink as he listened.

'Hello, Jack. You working?'

'I am. Absolutely filthy. Taking out fire damage. Can't talk long, I'm not in charge of this job and I was late coming in.'

'Can you have Mia this evening?'

Their daughter. 'Yeh. I'm not doing anything.'

'She has her grade 4 cello exam tomorrow. Can you make sure she practises tonight?'

'Isn't that up to her?'

'Give me strength, Jack. Are you a parent or not?'

He took another gulp of water. Best not to rise to her.

'I don't think you should force a kid,' he said carefully.

'Encourage, Jack. That's the word, encourage. Wouldn't you have liked to have learnt an instrument as a child?'

'Not the cello,' he said.

'It's a way in,' insisted Alison. 'It teaches you appreciation of music, notation, rhythm, dexterity. You can go on to other instruments.'

Jack couldn't argue; his ignorance was total. He tried to imagine himself, back in the day as a thirteen year old, walking down the street in Plaistow with a cello on his back. There'd be non-stop fights. It would've been smashed to bits. Anyone working hard, too keen or different got beaten up at Cumberland. Except at sport, that was valued. You'd get away with guitar but cellos were for nerds with thick glasses.

'OK,' he said. 'I shall crack the whip.'

'Encourage, Jack,' she insisted. 'In ten years' time she'll thank you.'

Ben had come out for a drink and was eyeing him.

'Got the message,' he said, aware the boss was watching. 'Must get back to work. See you.' He closed and looked to Ben with a half grin. 'My ex,' he said indicating the phone. 'My thirteen year old daughter is coming over tonight.' He laughed uncomfortably. 'I've got to make sure she practises her cello.'

Ben nodded. 'A fine thing, music. I'm learning the piano myself.'

'Are you now?' Genuinely surprised. 'How did that come about?'

'When my missus died. Three years ago now. Road accident.'

'Sorry to hear that.'

'Sally was just walking down the road and this car took the corner too quickly, swerved onto the pavement and hit her. Dead. Just forty-two. The cops came to the site I was working on. I couldn't believe it. We were going on holiday in a week.'

'That must've knocked the stuffing out of you. Hard times.'

'You can say that again. I couldn't sleep, almost suicidal. Insomnia is a curse when you're grieving. One day, three in the morning, I picked up Sally's music. She'd been learning the piano. For something to do, I plonked along the first page of the grade 1 book. 'Over the Hills and Far Away' it was. It took me over, filled my head. You might say 'Over the Hills and Far Away' saved my life.' He laughed. 'These sausage fingers. What a racket I was making! Going over and over. The neighbours complained. So I bought an electronic keyboard and headphones. Grade 1, grade 2. Those exams. You turn up to the place, and there's schoolkids waiting, confident as hell. I get so nervous, I'm shaking when I go in. You encourage that kid of yours, OK?'

'That's what my ex said. Encourage her. So I'd better, hadn't I? What grade you at?'

'Got my grade 4, working on 5.' He puffed his chest out, obviously pleased with himself. 'I've a music teacher now, over Wanstead. She's OK. Says it's good to have an adult, someone who wants to learn. What grade is your daughter?'

'She's got a grade 4 exam tomorrow. She was in a quartet, but that broke up. She's gone off it now. On her own. Hates scales.'

'Does she like jazz?'

'Don't know. She has to play classical for exams. Getting fed up with it.'

'Bring her over tonight. My place. We can do some jazz together. Me and you have a beer or two.'

'I don't drink.' Jack had to say that quick. Make it clear. No misunderstanding. 'Can't drink. Had trouble that way.'

'Got you, Jack. Coffee then. Come about half seven for a bit of music making. You can play the bongos.' Ben looked at his watch. 'I think we need a breakfast break.' He opened the door and called. 'Tony! Out here.'

Tony got down from the ladder and came outside, pulling away the mask as he came through the door. He was muscular in his ripped t-shirt, his sweaty arms sooty, carbon round his neck and face. Like three coal miners, thought Jack.

'We can't go to the café in this state,' said Ben looking at his hands and arms. 'So how about one of us gets some bacon sandwiches and tea? We have it out here.'

'I'll go,' said Tony quickly.

'You can't go like that.'

'I'll sponge my face and hands, got a jacket in the car. The Forest Café aren't fussy. Let's have some money.'

Chapter 2

Jack and Ben worked. It wasn't far to the Forest Café; Tony should be back in quarter of an hour, so a blast of work, then a replenishing bacon sandwich and tea. With the break coming, Jack remounted the high stepladder, bashing at the burnt steps. Keep going, the more done now, the less to do afterwards. Not long. Crack on.

The air was thick with carbon and ash, a bonfire smell. Pretend it's Guy Fawkes, fireworks, roast potatoes, and a penny for the guy. Though you wouldn't be thanked for a penny these days, besides which he hadn't seen a guy for years. Apart from the fireworks, Halloween had taken over. Hammer away, tell yourself tales, till Tony returns with breakfast.

A resident came through the garden door, an elderly black man in a blue woolly hat pushing a basket on wheels. Jack realised he'd come down the fire escape from one of the upstairs flats. The only way down with this staircase out of action.

'This is the devil's work,' he exclaimed, waving his hands at the dust and kicking away a piece of burnt wood. 'Apollyon in that house and the whore of Babylon there,' pointing out flats 1 and 2. 'We are entering the end of days. I warn them daily. I tell them: you have little time. Confess. Beg forgiveness. Do they listen? They do not. And the four riders are on their way. Lord have mercy on their souls.'

Ben and Jack stopped work for his passage through the hallway. The man gazed at the desolation as if it were

Calvary, with Jack up the ladder, one of the thieves on the cross, and Ben the other in what was left of the cupboard.

'What preparations are you making for Armageddon, sir?'

Ben took down his mask and stared in puzzlement at the man. 'I've a job to do. This hallway to clean up, and your stairs to put back. That's all this poor sinner can prepare for.'

'To admit to your sin is a beginning. A humbleness before the Lord. But it is not enough.' His voice had become soft and schoolteacherly. 'You must beg forgiveness in the name of our Saviour. Do it this very day, I beg of you. I have tried with the drug dealer there,' he pointed out flat 1, 'but he is of the devil's party. He will boil in oil for a billion years. I have tried with the whore,' he pointed out flat 2, 'but she will continue with her whoring until the beast devours her. Jezebel! Delilah! Betrayers of men since Eve's fall.'

'Didn't the serpent play some part?' suggested Jack.

'He chose the weaker one. Woman. Eve who brought sin onto her husband. And so wickedness entered the divine creation. All women are daughters of Eve, bearing children in pain and sin.'

'What about their brothers?' said Jack. 'I've come across a few sinners here and there.'

'Don't mock, philistine. You shall be smitten in the name of the Lord.'

'With the jawbone of an ass, I think it goes,' said Jack, remembering vaguely his Sunday School classes. 'But what will you do when the world doesn't end?'

'Oh ye of little faith!' His arms rose as if in supplication. 'The Anti-Christ is here with us. We have the gay plague, we have the United Nations and the hydrogen bomb. The ice caps are melting, Noah's animals are dying in their millions. How many signs do you need?'

'Six hundred and sixty six,' said Jack.

Ben scowled at him, giving a warning not to bait the man.

Suddenly the old man was coughing, holding his throat, head shaking back and forth. He leaned against the wall, his breathing slowing, a hand still pressing his neck.

'It's the fire of hell, demons scouring the earth on the final days. Repent! Repent.' Between coughs. 'You still have time.'

A fit of coughing all but overpowered him, but somehow he managed to push his basket through the dust of the hallway, one arm covering his mouth, and went out the open door. On the path, he stood gasping, hands on hips, body bending back and forth. He spat on the path, wiped his mouth with the back of his hand, spat again and looked, yelling words that Jack couldn't fully hear, making out sin, end of days, and fire something or other. He gathered the gist of it.

It was going to get bad, very bad, and he was doomed.

'Don't think he'll be making us a cup of tea,' said Ben watching the man head away. 'Where's Tony?'

'Gets busy, the café, about this time,' said Jack.

Ben was biting his knuckles. He looked up to Jack on the ladder. 'If you don't mind, Jack, I'm going to go and meet him. Might be having trouble carrying it all.'

'Don't want him spilling tea,' said Jack.

'Won't be long.' He patted Jack on the shoulder. 'You're in charge, mate.'

'Go get him. Stop him scoffing our sandwiches.'

Ben strode out with a wave. Jack went back to hammering off burnt steps. Several pieces fell to the ground. In charge now. Of what, exactly? The air of the hallway was a mist of particles, the floor covered in burnt wood, nails, and bits of plaster. He couldn't do much about the air, but the floor was a danger to any resident coming through. He put down his club hammer and took up the broom. As he swept, he thought, why am I the only one working? The boss and his son wandering the streets.

The way it was on site, he knew well enough, the foreman away, the workers slowed up. But then again, he had been late this morning. Jack continued sweeping a clear pathway through the hall, pushing the larger pieces of timber and metal against the wall, out of the way.

That was done, the rubbish against one wall, but really they needed a skip to fill as they went along. Except he wasn't in charge, no matter what Ben said. And a skip was coming in the afternoon.

He could do with that tea and bacon sandwich. The two of them out, it reminded him of a kid's story book, the sort he would read to Mia when she was small. Mr Builder goes to the shop, when he doesn't come back Mr Brickie goes to find him, Mr Chippy and Mr Sparks wait, and when they don't come back Chippy sets off in turn. And when he doesn't come back...

But Jack was staying put. Let the big bad wolf get them.

He went outside, sat on the step and took a drink of water. The metal cups were labelled in red paint: A, B and C. He was C. Ben and Tony were A and B. Stick to your own spit, Tony had told him. Sound hygiene.

All he'd had was a slice of bread and jam before leaving in the morning, too late rising for anything else. Must shop this evening, with Mia coming over. He could leave her practising the cello. Though would she, if he wasn't there? Like him, sitting on the step with the boss gone.

The way of the world.

Ben had invited him over. Jack wasn't sure he wanted to go, but this job could last a month. So he'd better be there. Besides, Ben was OK. Jack had been surprised with him talking about the death of his wife. Such personal stuff wasn't normal on site, so soon. And how he'd got into playing the piano. Just goes to show, you can't judge a man by his overalls. Not every builder goes straight to the pub after work and goes home and beats up the wife. Not that such men didn't exist, but he'd worked with a Latvian who spoke four languages, a bricklayer who'd sailed on his own to Norway.

And there was that Russian, a nuclear physicist, would you believe, who'd been ordered to assist with the clean up of Chernobyl. A gang of builders had been up on the roof having lunch and the Russian told his tales. How he'd refused to go to the nuclear site and been told that he'd never work in the nuclear industry again. 'Sawdust is better than radiation,' he told Jack. Adding that every one of his colleagues who'd obeyed had died of cancer within ten years.

A door opened, one of the two flats in the hallway. A young woman came out holding a small plunger. She flapped at the dust, saw him on the step and came down the passage, her flip-flops slapping on the concrete floor. She was on the small side, slim, her hair dark brown and frizzy. Her jeans were torn at the knee, a fashion Jack thought daft. Why spoil good clothes?

She stood over him, waving the plunger, 'This is useless. I wonder if you'd have a bigger one.'

'Mine's bigger than yours,' he said.

She blew a raspberry at him. Her face was freckled.

'Show me it then.'

Chapter 3

As Ben walked down Forest Lane, he wiped his face and neck with the wet sponge he'd taken from the site. He was grimy, just moving the dirt down to his neck in a tide line, and passing the playground and buildings of Forest Gate school, much improved, they said, since he'd gone there. Couldn't be worse. On the other side, a train was whooshing through, behind the high wall that hid the station platforms from the street. Must be an express for Ipswich or Norwich.

One time at the school, they'd done a project. And gone onto Forest Gate platform, the whole class with clipboards, and noted the destinations of the trains. The stoppers and those that disdained the small station.

Ben's shoulders were hunched as he rapidly crossed the road to the station entrance, not going the extra thirty yards to the clock and horse font where the crossing was. Everyone crossed here, all the kids from school, this was where the crossing should be. Ben passed the station front with its red brick and stacked portakabins. Would they ever finish the building work? Going on for two years or more. Though as a builder, he could see the problem of working when the station had to be open all week for commuters.

But they seemed to have a lot of workers and not much happening. Slack foreman, slack boss, all the same, these big contracts. The never ending Crossrail. Offering fast trains to the West End and Heathrow, one day, never.

Woodgrange Road was busy with cars and buses which was why he was walking. No parking anyway. A police siren sounded, its urgent call and flashing blue light sending all traffic to the side of the road as two cars sped through.

Someone was for it.

Ben went into the Forest Café. A greasy spoon of a place, fine for a tea break or lunch. Cheap. He walked through to the far end. There were a couple of builders he knew, eating eggs on toast, a bacon sandwich. They offered him a place at their table. He shook his head.

'I'm looking for Tony. You seen him?'

'He was here half an hour ago!' cried Livy, behind the counter, in white overalls slapping burgers in a pan. 'He ordered three teas, three bacon sandwiches. And hasn't come back for them.' He turned and picked up a cardboard tray with the sandwiches in paper bags and plastic cups with lids. 'Here. The tea's well cold. Who's going to pay for it?'

Ben took out his wallet. Opening it, he looked at the thin wedge of notes, hesitated and pulled out a ten pound note and handed it over.

'Sorry about that,' said Ben. 'Something turned up. Keep the change.'

The man took the money. 'Do you want the food?'

'No. Do what you want with it.'

Giving no explanation, Ben turned and headed out the door and down the high street. Another tenner gone. Jack had had no change and so had given Tony a tenner, he'd given him another himself. And with the tenner just handed over, that was thirty quid gone. Whistle for that. Ben had wondered at his son's eagerness, but you always hope. Only up the road and back, surely he'd be OK?

Fat chance.

He popped into Paddy Power. On one of the large, high up screens, horses were being led round the paddock, a commentary giving names, riders and odds. Ben went to the end of the shop, passing the manager in her glass kiosk. An

Asian man was on the fixed odds betting machine, pumping in pound coins and setting the digital roulette wheel running. Not Tony though.

Out of the shop and into William Hill, another betting office, all built to the same pattern, a long room with a row of screens above head height, betting odds plastered on the wall, a woman, nearly always a woman in the kiosk. In this shop, a favourite with black men, their home from home, a group watching a race, an old man reading a racing paper.

On to BetFred. Five betting shops on this small stretch. Taking bread out of the mouths of wives and children, emptying dinner tables and fridges, a prime cause of evictions. Though she'd kicked him out beforehand, Tony's wife. Who could blame her?

Now Ben was lumbered with him. Promised Sally he'd look after Tony.

Twenty five years old, married, and back home again.

As he strode down the pavement, he had eyes only for his son. Not seeing the chicken shops, competing with the betting shops in number. The debate, when a shop closed, which would it be next. Fast food or fast bets? Not seeing the fancy curtain shop with no prices on anything, the luggage shop where the Asian man looked so miserable amidst the walls of suitcases and rucksacks. No eyes for pedestrians: men in turbans, women in burqas, black, white, brown, a melange of language in the exhaust filled air. Eastern Europeans, Asian, English of all ilk, shadows without features.

The shame of it. Jack had given his son a tenner, never mind the one he himself had given him. And Tony had gone off with it and Ben knew where he'd go and simply hoped he wouldn't. Always less bearable when witnessed. It was one thing him knowing, another others seeing what should have stayed in the family. Thank God Sally wasn't here. How would she have dealt with her son?

And Jack left waiting at the site for his bacon sandwich. On his own, working. That's no way to do things. You don't take on a guy and leave him there after a couple of hours. You have an obligation. Be fair, or word would get out.

So where to go now? He stopped and considered. Hunt down Tony, wherever he might be, or get the grub himself? Make up some story for Jack. Or just say what was what. It was too obvious anyway.

And there he was, Tony. Coming out of a betting office, across the road, in handcuffs between two policemen.

Chapter 4

Jack returned to Heidi's flat with a small pump. The kitchen was medium-sized with a view out to the back garden from which Jack could see the metal fire escape with a young man coming noisily down. For furniture, there was a small table with two chairs, the usual units, a double sink, a dishwasher, a cooker and large fridge. It was tidier than his own place. Heidi had put the kettle on and had bread in the toaster.

At least he'd get something to eat here. Almost lunchtime anyway. Some job, the Wilsons, father and son, disappearing on him.

The pump was his own adaptation of a car foot-pump, to which he'd added a length of hose with a plunger end. He'd seen a Latvian plumber use one and made one for himself. A blocked sink was usually caused by food waste trapped in the U-bend. Sometimes a plunger could force it through, but often couldn't. The foot pump gave extra force. If it didn't work then the U-bend had to be removed which would be a bigger job than he could do now, what with Ben paying for his time. Though he could do it after work, if needs be.

'This gadget will either work,' he said, 'or it won't.'

'I knew that before you said it,' she said with a smile that lifted her freckled cheeks. She pulled the toast from the toaster and put the slices on a plate.

'It was rather obvious,' he admitted. 'Self protection.' He was watching her butter the bread, aware of his own blackened hands and face. But she had invited him in, his footprints staining the floor tiles. 'Anyway, it will either force the blockage through or the U-bend has to be taken off. And cleared. And I haven't got time for that as my boss will be back any minute and will want to know what I'm doing here.'

'Then stop jabbering,' she said, then reflected at her tone. 'That wasn't meant to be rude, but I do want my sink fixed. And don't want to get you in trouble.'

'Appreciated,' he said.

The sink was empty apart from a few inches of scummy water. Jack put the plunger end over the plug hole and the foot pump on the floor. And began rapidly depressing the pump with his foot. The liquid in the waste pipe gurgled as Jack levered up and down. And then suddenly with a gurgle, it was free. He took up the plunger end, and the water in the sink ran down the plughole.

'Done!'

She clapped her hands. 'Marvellous! Thank you, thank you.'

He took out the pump. 'I'm going to put this away before the boss knows what I've been up to. He thinks I'm working away on the hallway. Can you bring the tea and toast outside?'

'Give me a few minutes,' she said. 'Do you like Marmite?'

'Love it.'

Jack left her, pleased with the work. Attractive woman, seemed to live on her own from what he could see. Tea and toast coming, the boss not back yet. All was right with the world.

He locked the pump in the van, evidence of his moon-lighting hidden away. Though if he knew Ben better, would he really object to five minutes off from the job? But he was the new boy, lots he didn't know about his boss. Like where he was.

By the front step, he poured water into a bucket and did a crude washing of his hands. No soap. There was some in his van but he couldn't be bothered to go back for it. No towel. He wiped his hands on his overalls. His face was filthy but he wasn't touching that. Ben had taken the sponge to wherever father and son were now. Failing the bacon sandwich, he at least was promised tea and toast. And some pleasant company.

What had happened to them? Why had Ben been so concerned? Drink, drugs, gambling, a woman. A multiple choice question. Tick whichever is applicable.

A shuffling sound behind him told him someone was coming down the hallway. Heidi? No, but a woman in a black burqa, a narrow slit for her eyes, carrying a shopping bag. Must be an upstairs tenant.

'Sorry about the dust,' he said as she came through.

'Can't be helped,' she said and stopped. He was surprised that she'd replied. A local accent too. She was looking at him; he wasn't sure of the etiquette, just knew he shouldn't stare. 'Those kids and their drugs,' she went on. 'I am sure it was. Could have killed us all.'

'Good job the fire brigade were quick,' he said.

'Lucky for us. They saved us,' she said. 'I must get to the shops. When my daughter comes home, we'll make you some tea.'

'Always appreciate a cuppa, Missus.'

'Mrs Nawaz. And you are?'

'I'm Jack,' he said. 'There's three of us working here, but the other two are at the café.'

'And they left you all alone?' She snorted. 'Not fair.'

'They'll be back soon,' he said, excusing his colleagues. 'I'm sure.'

He wasn't, of course. Though he was growing less concerned about their delay, especially now as he saw Heidi coming out of her flat with a tray. She stepped rapidly through the hallway in her flat shoes. He wondered if she'd been a waitress.

'Good morning, Mrs Nawaz. Jack fixed my blocked sink.'

'I see you've got some tea, Jack. You see, you're valued. Good morning, Heidi. Not working today?'

'I'll be at the hospital tomorrow.'

'So a nurse tomorrow. Variety is the spice of life, they say. Must go. Lots to do. Bye bye.'

And she set off down the path. Heidi put the tray down on the path before Jack. It had two mugs of tea and a couple of slices of toast.

'What was that about 'a nurse tomorrow'?'

'A private joke we have. It'll take too long to explain,' she said. 'The toast is for you. And a cuppa. One minute.'

She went back inside. More? he thought, and took up a mug and sipped. A long time coming, this cuppa, but so welcoming. The toast was warm and crunchy, the sharp Marmite molten in the butter. A small bite of heaven.

A nurse tomorrow, he mused, and what the day after?

Heidi returned with two folding chairs. She unfolded one.

'There. Sit.'

He hesitated. 'I'll get it filthy.'

She flapped away his reluctance. 'It'll wash off. Be comfortable. You did me a favour.'

Jack sat down on the chair, the plate of toast in his lap, a mug of tea in his hand. And wondered what Ben might say, if he ever returned. Though he couldn't complain, having left Jack for, must be an hour now.

'How long have you lived here?' he said.

'Five months,' she said. She had unfolded the other chair and was sitting in it with her tea. 'I needed to live local. I'm a nurse at Newham University Hospital.'

He smiled, locals called it Newham General, the University bit sounded poncy.

'How'd you get a Council flat?' he said. 'Two bedrooms too.'

She bit her lip. And he knew he shouldn't have asked. He could guess the reply anyway. Only been here five months. Single. She wouldn't get a council flat.

'You moonlight as an inspector for the Council?'

'Forget it. It's not my business.'

'I had to live somewhere,' she protested as she sipped her tea. 'There were two of us. Another nurse. She left last week. I have to get someone else as I can't afford it on my own.' She looked him in the eye. 'I don't need your approval.'

He shrugged. 'Probably do the same myself in your situation. As you say, got to live somewhere. Housing shortage. It's all a racket wherever you look.'

'It's not cheap,' she said.

'Wouldn't be. The tenant's making money out of you.' He smiled as he took a bite of toast. 'Anything else you want to confess while we are at it?'

'I didn't confess. You got it out of me. I'm not the legal tenant. That's not a criminal offence. My landlord, he's the one guilty, I'm just paying him too much. And I'm out any time the Council finds out the tenant is illegally subletting. Going to tell them?'

'None of my business.'

He wished he'd never started on this route. Talked about films or music. She had to live somewhere.

'Now your turn,' she said, her hands on her knees pressing forward. 'Confess something.'

He put down his mug. 'Must I?'

'Yes,' she said. 'Or I'll hate you.'

Jack blew out a long breath. He'd started it. Payment was due.

'I had, I mean have, a problem with alcohol,' he said. He'd grown good at confessing this one, from sessions at Alcohol Halt where the mantra was 'tell people'.

'So my wife kicked me out and divorced me,' he went on.

'Very sensible of her. How long ago?'

'Three years or so back. I don't drink now.'

They didn't talk for a while. Absorbing what he'd said and the effects of it. Jack automatically finished the toast without noticing he was eating. He put down the empty cup.

'We can talk about the weather now,' she said.

'Might rain tonight,' he said. 'Though could be clear tomorrow. Or the other way round.' He gave a short laugh, still uncomfortable after his admission. 'You got a boy-friend?'

'Why do you want to know?'

'I've got a friend who'd like to ask you out.'

'I've got a friend who'd like to ask you out.'

They laughed.

She said, 'I could invite you for a meal but I won't.'

'What have I done?' Knowing his inquisition hadn't helped.

'This lot, they gossip.' She indicated up and down the housing block. 'They think I have too many boyfriends.'

'Do you?'

'That would be telling.'

'You play the field?'

'I chucked the last. Only he won't give up. A creep.' She shivered. 'He was a real octopus. Xavier, that's his name. A Spanish waiter.'

'Xavier the Octopus,' mused Jack. 'Sounds like a kids' picture book.'

'I won't be reading it.'

'Octopuses are supposed to be intelligent.'

'Must've been a squid then. Had eight arms, I know that.'

'My place then?'

'Can you cook?'

'I do an excellent takeaway.'

'Can you do a Moon House Special?'

'I could have one on the table seven thirty tomorrow night.'

He put his hand on hers and instantly retracted at the sight of Ben coming up the path carrying a small bag. Main business done, he reflected. And don't be a Xavier. Take it slow, if she gives you time.

You never can tell.

'Your sandwich, Jack.' Ben held up the bag. Jack took it from him. 'And your change. Sorry it's been an age.' He delved in his pocket and sorted out a note and some silver which he handed over.

'Heidi made me tea,' said Jack.

'He was working non-stop, all on his own,' she said. 'I felt sorry for him.'

'Kind of you, Miss.' Ben was obviously flustered. 'I didn't mean to leave you like that.'

'Where's Tony?'

Ben's hands flew to his neck, overwhelmed. 'He's been arrested. I can't cope with him and this job. It's on a tight margin. Delay by a day and I lose money. I've got a skip coming soon.' He shook his head and sighed. 'And I have to go to the police station.'

'What's he done?' said Jack.

'Assaulted the manager of a betting office. I must get him a lawyer, but it's an open and shut case. There's witnesses, they told me, CCTV...' He threw up his hands. 'What's the point of spending money on a lawyer? Tell me that.'

'Maybe he just went crazy,' said Heidi.

'Why would he do that?'

'I don't know. I should shut up.'

'Yes, you should,' Ben said sharply. Then held his hands up. 'Sorry, sorry, Miss. I shouldn't be attacking you. I'm in a mood. It's not as if you've done anything. Sorry.'

'It's OK,' said Heidi. 'You're stressed and I spoke out of turn.'

'No,' he said, 'maybe a lawyer can do something. Things I haven't thought of. I'm a builder. What do I know about the law? Besides, I didn't see what happened. It could be better than I think.' He turned to Jack. 'I've got to go to the cop shop. You're in charge. The skip might come before I get back...'

'No problem,' said Jack. 'You get off. I'll carry on with the demolition.'

'Good man.'

Ben patted him on the shoulder, stopped as if to speak, his hand still held, but shook his head as if he'd lost the art of speech. He turned and hurried down the path.

Chapter 5

Heidi had returned to her flat, Ben was off searching for his errant son, leaving Jack working on his own. An odd state of affairs, he reflected. But it wasn't working out badly. Heidi had given him breakfast and a chat, so a better break than he'd have had with Ben and Tony. A date tomorrow night? Was that fixed up or not? They'd almost got there and Ben came.

She hadn't quite accepted. Or had she? He'd better get it straight. Plenty of time. Now he could work at his own pace. His lateness this morning was forgotten; it wasn't on the scale compared with Tony's escapade.

The passageway was becoming precarious with timber, bent railings, and plaster fragments refusing to lie against the walls. A building inspector would halt the work immediately.

The skip was needed.

If this had been his job, he'd have had the skip here first thing. That way the debris could have been carted straight onto it. Working like this meant moving everything twice. Once against the wall, and then into a wheelbarrow and outside and into the skip. With the skip here, you could heave it straight into a barrow and straight out. But it wasn't his job, he was a paid hand, a position he didn't relish, never liked having a boss, but necessity called the tune. On the other hand, there were advantages in not rushing the job, the main one being that Ben was paying him for the hours he worked. Moving the debris twice spun out the work, giving him more time on the job. So why complain?

He just didn't like wasting time and effort. Working mostly for himself, he would try to do things as efficiently as possible. That's how you made money on a job. Ben was no bloated capitalist, just a small contractor working on a tight price. But he hadn't thought this out, maybe all the worry with Tony had caused him to take his eye off the ball. Working so inefficiently, neither Ben or Tony here, Jack might be earning money but Ben was losing it.

You can't run a job like this with only one worker. Not his problem. All he could do was get on with it. Earn his keep. When he'd arrived first thing and seen the condition of the hall, he'd almost walked away. But being broke concentrated his mind. The three of them could clear the debris in a day or two. That had been his thinking. Grin and bear it. Shovel and hack, drink plenty of water. But now he was alone, in charge of the dust.

Jack had hardly spoken to Tony. Seemed OK first thing. He was the gaffer's son and had gone off with their breakfast money. And now his dad was off trying to keep him out of jail. What a change round! Jack had come in late, been admonished, and three hours later he was the man in charge.

He'd opened front and back doors, using rubble to keep the doors wide and to let fresh air in and the dusty air out. Workwise, he'd devised a system: ten minutes on, five off. He set his phone to ring for the breaks. At the end of ten minutes' graft, he would step outside, pull down his mask and suck in the fresh air. And drink. Though carefully. It wasn't thirst, but a need to swill out his throat. And he didn't want to be bursting for a pee every five minutes. He could call on Heidi at a pinch but he'd noted she wasn't too happy at the dirty towel he'd left in her bathroom. It wouldn't do to ask again, not if she was coming over tomorrow night. Drink sparingly, and go home lunchtime. Soon enough. It was only a short drive which was the advantage of these local jobs. Maybe walk.

The day was warm, the sky blue with patches of cumulus cloud, giving him five minutes of sunlight each time he freed himself from the cavern. The system broke the job into manageable chunks, carrot and stick. He need only think as far as the next break.

He'd been working his on-off system maybe five times when he came across the metal box. It was on the floor of the cupboard and had been covered in ash and burnt timber. The ash was wet from the firefighters' hoses. Most of the water had been swished away by Council workers when they'd come after the fire, but the deeper ash was soggy.

The box was shut tight, the size of a thick paperback, blackened with soot, most of the paint burnt off. Curious, he took the box outside into the light. There, he sat on the step and worked at prising off the lid. Likely its contents would be disappointing, a cleaning product. But the fact of it being closed so tight teased his curiosity.

It had got to him now, having started. Wasn't there some ancient Greek woman, what was her name, he'd come across her when looking up the origin of constellation names, most came from Greek myths, she'd been told not to open a box. Well, that's a tempter. She didn't, but her husband did. And out came all the troubles of the world. What was her name? Jack went through the alphabet. A for Andromeda, no, she was on a rock, rescued by Perseus, two constellations next to each other. B for Betelgeuse the Red Giant, but that was Arabic and not a constellation anyway. Cassiopeia, the big W pointing to the Pole Star. Pandora! That was it. Pandora's Box. Yes, yes, yes. He was quite triumphant. He felt like phoning Alison, yelling at her, you may read the Guardian but I'm not just a know nothing builder!

Jack laughed at his inward boasting to his ex. Somewhat too late for that. He shook the tin. Nothing rattled, but the thought of all the troubles of the world made him pause.

And then he berated himself for giving in to superstition. Open the damn thing, there was no one here to say otherwise. Give it some thump.

A couple of blows with a screwdriver and hammer dented the tin box. Several more belts and he was able to lever off the lid.

No troubles flew out. Or at least none that he could see. The inside was nearly full of a brown, waxy substance, obviously melted in the fire and then re-solidified. He sniffed it. A strong, resinous smell. Furniture polish? But why on earth would you have it in the hallway cupboard? What was there to polish?

Drugs, then. The youngsters smoked them in the hallway, maybe dealt them too. Quite a stash, if it was. Not marijuana, he knew that sweetish smell. But wasn't familiar with much else. For all he knew, it could be crack, opium, heroin or heaven knows what else that had been concocted to befuddle the human mind. Of course, it could be a cleaning product. He'd look a prize idiot taking it to the police station, to be told it was car wax.

Jack considered what to do with it. He could throw it in the skip when it came or hand it in to the police and chance their ridicule. For want of a decision, he put it in a bucket outside the door, and tipped over it a shovel full of rubble. It seemed a little excessive, Ben might laugh at him for his secrecy. He was about to pull it out of the bucket, but do exactly what with it?

Leave it and decide later.

When he came back into the hall, a black youngster, thin with long limbs and dreadlocks, nineteen or so, was looking in what had been the cupboard. He was kicking the rubble, moving boards.

'Hey, what you up to?' called Jack.

The youth looked at him sullenly, shifting his hair out of his eyes. He was about the same height as Jack, wearing a red t-shirt patterned with a black, aggressive, helmeted head, who Jack recognised as Judge Dredd.

'I left something here,' said the youngster morosely.

'Care to tell me what?'

The young man shrugged, kicking some burnt boards aside. 'Just something. I live up there.' He indicated over what was left of the burnt staircase with his thumb. 'Our flat is too crowded to keep things in.' He kneeled down and threw some broken wood aside. And grimaced as sticky ash stuck to his finger. He turned and peered at Jack. 'You sure you haven't found anything?'

'Anything left here, the fire would have burnt.'

The young man was about to say something but changed his mind. He looked about him.

'Sorry about the mess,' he said. 'I'll tidy it up for you.'

'No, leave it,' said Jack. 'You'll make yourself filthy. I'll do it.'

'Didn't mean to make a mess. But I lost me thing. You know?'

'What's your name?'

'Sol. What's yours?'

'Jack.'

'You wouldn't be holding back on me, Jack?'

'Not me.' Though knowing that he was, being fairly certain what the youngster was after.

Sol scowled. 'There's been so many people down here. Fire brigade, then the Council cleaning up and now you lot.' He grinned, having it seemed two modes which switched in and out like rain and fine weather figures. 'It's gonna take ages with just you.'

Jack's own thoughts exactly, but he said, 'The others have gone for a tea break.'

Sol had gone back to the search, walking about the space. He stopped and shook his head despondently.

'There's gonna be trouble, I know it. I got to go places. See ya.'

A switch to grin phase, but lacking pleasantry. And he was off, in a rangy prance.

Jack tidied up for a few minutes. When he was sure Sol had gone, Jack went outside. He took the bucket with the box buried in it under rubble to his van. He looked up and down the road making sure no one was about. Then took the box out and put it in his van, under a decorating sheet.

He thought about the contents as he returned to the hallway. What had he got himself involved in? What trouble did the youngster mean? There are dangerous people involved in drugs. But he couldn't just hand over a tin full of them to a teenager.

Half an hour later, the large skip came, high on the back of a lorry. Jack went out to the roadside. It was clear the skip needed room by the kerb and the closest place was taken up with his van.

'I'll move my van,' he called to the driver.

The driver waved and backed up to give him space to get out. Jack had to drive some way up the road to find a new parking spot. As he walked back, the skip was being lowered to the roadside. The driver was wasting no time. And there was Ben walking rapidly towards it.

The two of them watched the skip come down slowly, powered by the hydraulics of the lorry's crane.

'How did it go at the cop shop?' said Jack, as they watched the driver take the chains off.

'I got Tony a solicitor and had to wait for him. Sorry I've been so long, but I had to talk to the solicitor to find out where Tony stood. He says he'll try to get bail, but is sure the police will oppose it as Tony has a record.'

'What's he done before?'

'He was in a gang. The FG Crew they called themselves. Fights and drugs, and I don't know what else. He got a year inside for grievous bodily harm. He was drunk and hit a guy with a bottle, smacked a copper too. Stupid. When he got out, I gave him a job. To keep him straight, to keep him away from the gang. He's been alright for eight months...' He stopped, opening his hands in a helpless gesture. 'He's not a bad bloke, just impulsive.' He shrugged. 'Nothing more I can do for him now.'

The skip was down, chains removed, the driver was impatient to be away as a couple of vehicles were stuck behind his lorry, hooting to get by. Ben signed the paperwork, and the driver climbed back in his cab.

'Let's fill it up,' said Ben, indicating the skip.

'How long we got it for?'

'Two days. Today we get the stairs and cupboard out, start stripping the plaster on the walls and ceiling, finish it tomorrow, maybe afternoon. I was hoping in the morning, but with just the two of us, and the time I've lost...' He shrugged. 'Can't be done. You up for any overtime tonight?'

'Can't do it. My daughter's coming over.'

'Of course, you told me. I fixed up you and her coming over to do some jazz with me. Forgot.'

'You still in the mood?'

'I need it. Forget Tony for an hour. I'll get us a cake.'

Jack took his wheelbarrow out of the van, Ben brought one from his. And they began loading. The work was a relief to Jack, making him feel they were getting somewhere. They stacked burnt timbers onto wheelbarrows and ferried them to the skip. Then the two of them would lift the barrow and heave the contents in. Then back for more.

They were contemplating stopping for lunch when the police arrived.

Chapter 6

Jack was in the hallway, loading timber onto a wheelbarrow, when they came in two cars. In the first were three plain clothes police. One of them was Fayyad, a school friend of his, a detective sergeant at Forest Gate police station. If he'd have been on his own, Jack would have asked him what was happening, but intimidated by the number, he felt it best to wait and see.

With Fayyad were two other plain clothes officers, both women. He'd seen them with Fayyad before, names forgotten, but the older woman he knew was Fayyad's boss, quite high up at the station. From the other car alighted two uniformed police officers who followed the plain clothes officers into the hallway.

'Jack, isn't it?' said the senior officer.

'Yes,' he said.

'Hardly recognised you, so blacked up. I'm Detective Superintendent Nikki Martin if you recall, and this is DS Kamani who I think you know...'

Jack was impressed that she remembered him, and his relationship with Fayyad.

'Fayyad and I were at Cumberland School,' he said. 'And you're Hayley,' he said to the tall plain clothes woman, as it flashed to him who she was.

'Dirty job you've got here,' said Hayley, looking around at the blackened walls.

'Not pleasant,' he said.

'You have to leave the hallway, I'm afraid,' said Nikki. 'Right away.'

'For how long?'

'Depends what we find in flat 1.' She indicated the door of the flat, the one opposite Heidi's. 'We have information,' went on Nikki. 'Might be erroneous. If so, you can come straight back. On the other hand if it's correct, we'll be here some time. And this hallway will be out of bounds to everyone except residents.'

Jack registered the vagueness of 'some time'. Could mean a day, several days. Longer? What on earth had been going on in the flat, if the information was correct? Enough to bring five cops, including Madam Bigshoes.

'So I'd be obliged if you go outside now,' she added. She smiled, which was friendly but assertive.

Jack nodded and went for the wheelbarrow handles, when Nikki put a hand on his shoulder.

'Leave that, if you please,' she said sharply. 'And any tools.'

Jack looked about the hallway, about to complain, but saw Fayyad shaking his head. Alongside, he noted a uniformed police officer had a small metal ram in readiness. Not the time to worry about a wheelbarrow and tools. This was serious business.

Jack left the hallway without protest.

Outside on the path, Ben was by his wheelbarrow, peering in.

'What's going on?' he said in a hushed voice.

'We've got to stop work,' said Jack. 'Something's going on in flat 1. That's all I know.'

Ben threw his gloves in the wheelbarrow. 'That's all we need, cops on the rampage. This job is jinxed. Never liked fire damage. Should've known, this place.'

Known what, thought Jack. That flat 1 had something to do with the fire damage? Did he really know something? Or was it just the talk of a frustrated small contractor?

They watched as Nikki rang the bell of the flat. Once, then after about five seconds, three times. Jack wondered whether the bell was working. Should be, as being Council, it would be mains powered rather than battery. No response. Nikki pummelled the door with her fists. Jack winced; she must have tough hands to be able to give such a pounding. Martial arts maybe. She waited a while and then bent to her knees and called through the letterbox.

'Police! Open up. Or we'll break down the door.'

Several times she shouted the order. Across the hallway, Heidi's door opened. She came out and was ordered back in by Fayyad. She caught Jack's eye and went in with reluctance.

Nikki stood back from the door. She nodded to the uniformed officer with the ram. The other officers gave him space, as he began smashing at the door around the lock. The sharp banging of the ram echoed round the hallway, bringing spectators from above, like gallery seating, held back from the stalls by the removed staircase.

'If the door didn't need replacing, it does now,' said Ben watching the officer rhythmically hammering away at the frame and door.

Through the thumping, Jack was thinking ahead. If the police found nothing inside, they'd need to seal the door, Ben being on the spot would get the work, but if they found something as Nikki had indicated... And what might that be? A drug haul, money, a body? Then he and Ben would be out of work as Nikki had indicated. The flat and hall would be a crime scene.

He kept his thoughts to himself. Why panic Ben when it could be a false alarm? But the police must have sound intelligence to be smashing the door in. Though mistakes are made. He watched, half wishing for the thrill of something sensational, so he could tell the world, but more sensibly wanting a damp squib so he'd stay employed.

The frame's wood was splintering, the lock buckling, as the officer bashed on with the ram, hitting at the weaknesses. The door post caved, and, all at once, the door sprung open.

The policeman put down the ram. Nikki cautiously went to the open door. She kicked it wide open and called in, 'Police! Anyone in there? Come out immediately. Police. You will not be harmed. Come out!'

There was no response. She repeated her order.

Nikki said something inaudible to Fayyad who handed her a fat, plastic package. He had one himself. They ripped it open and took out paper coveralls which the two officers swiftly pulled over their clothing. They covered their heads with the hood, put overshoes over their footwear, and completed the cover up with plastic gloves.

Suitably sinister in their baggy gear, the two officers went into the flat. Anyone inside, if there was anyone hiding under the bed, would be scared out of their wits to see abominable snowmen coming for them.

The flat was probably the same set up as Heidi's, thought Jack: two bedrooms, a sitting room, a kitchen, and a bathroom. The police outside peered down the hallway, taking care not to step over the threshold to avoid contamination. Nikki and Fayyad were shouting out as they went from room to room. Jack could hear but was too far to make out all the words.

After a minute or so, Fayyad and Nikki came out.

'There's a body in the kitchen,' she said. 'Contact CSI, Hayley. This is now a crime scene.'

Chapter 7

'I'll pay you for today's work,' said Ben.

They were at Jack's place which was only a short drive from the site. The police had made it clear they had to be completely off the premises. Tools and wheelbarrows had to be left, nor were they allowed to wash from their bucket before leaving.

'Sorry, Jack,' Fayyad had said, 'but you might be sluicing away evidence.'

'And what might that be?'

'Don't know,' said Fayyad, 'but you can't test what isn't there.'

To which there could be no answer. The crime scene investigation took precedence. A police officer took his and Ben's fingerprints with his handheld machine.

'For elimination purposes,' said Fayyad. 'They will be destroyed after the investigation.'

Ben and Jack then left, leaving behind two wheelbarrows, shovels, hammers, saws, cold chisels, and a broom. The area was taped off, with a uniformed policeman allowing only residents and police beyond the tape.

On arriving at his flat, Jack had offered Ben first use of his bathroom, but Ben declined.

'It's your place,' he said.

Jack washed his hands and face, leaving a grubby towel for Ben. No matter; they were builders, and Ben wouldn't expect the soft towels of a posh hotel. After Ben left, Jack would have a shower, wash his overalls too, as he wouldn't be working for a day or two. Surely no longer?

He made tea and put the bacon sandwich in the microwave. He'd saved it from earlier and offered Ben half.

'I'm not hungry, Jack.'

There was no point insisting, Ben was flattened by the events of the morning, in no state to note the messiness of the kitchen, with two days of dishes in the sink and dirty pots on the stove.

'They say misfortune comes in threes,' he said, his chin in his hands over the table. 'Tony in the nick, this job going down the tubes... I'm waiting for the third.'

Neither spoke for a while. Jack munched the sandwich. He had nothing comforting to say on the matter of Ben's misfortune. Tony was in custody, fact. The site was a crime scene, fact. Matters were out of their hands. Jack needed to juggle his own finances; Tony wasn't his affair, nor was he responsible for the job.

'I wonder who the body is,' he said at last.

'At least dead, nothing worse can happen to him.'

'Or her,' said Jack.

Though it was pointless speculating. But he'd noted Ben had immediately said 'him'. Jack mentally shook himself. Do not assume. He wasn't a cop. Ben was simply engaging in male chivalry, not wanting to think of a dead woman.

'They must be thinking murder,' he mused, considering the haste at which they'd been moved off site. 'Crime scene, CSI on the way, fingerprints, DNA and whatnot.'

'Sorry, Jack. I can't think about it.' Ben waved a hand as if to halt his thoughts. 'Someone dead who I don't know from Adam. It means nothing to me.'

'It's stopping us working.'

'That's a pain in the neck. Money flowing out, nothing coming in. Tony's solicitor is going to cost a packet, though heaven knows what he can do.' He shook his fists in frustration. 'I've a half filled skip that's supposed to be removed late tomorrow. How can they say that's part of the crime scene?'

'Might be something in it,' said Jack. He'd finished the bacon sandwich and wiped his hands on a grubby tea towel.

'It's just burnt timber and rubble.'

'It's the way they work,' said Jack. 'They don't believe anyone.' Fayyad had told him this when he'd gone to visit him and his family in Ilford. 'The slightest thing might turn out to be evidence.'

'And our tools,' exclaimed Ben. 'Do they think I clobbered whoever with a shovel?'

'Such things happen.'

Ben rose. 'Yeh, maybe. I don't know. They've got their job. I just wish we had ours. Thanks for the tea. I've got to go. Must check my bank account. See if I've enough before the bailiffs come round.' He halted at the kitchen door and turned. 'You don't have to come tonight. I'll be miserable company.'

Jack thought so too, but had already committed himself. Though he was dragging Mia into a heavy evening. He'd bribe her with something, and leave as early as he could. But there was still work on offer when the cops finished. And Ben was the boss.

'We'll be there,' he said. 'Cheer you up.'

Ben left. Jack showered. Then threw his dirty clothing in the machine. While it washed, he went out to the shop.

Chapter 8

Mia entered, bowed down with the cello on her back and school bag on her front. She slipped off the bag and dropped it on the sofa as if it were so much garbage. More carefully she took off the cello, several times shrugging her neck and shoulders to ease them. And laid the instrument against the wall, out of the way.

Jack was at the sitting room table, as she came in, working at his laptop. He was clean, hair wispy from the shower. The washing machine in the kitchen was rumbling away. He'd been checking his bank account and it told him what he already knew; his overdraft was being eaten up too quickly. He could get by for a week maybe, which was why the job mattered. But Ben's gloom was a worry. How bad were his financial troubles? Jack had been on a job a few years back where he and the other workers had turned up for work in the morning, and found the gate padlocked. The contractor had gone bankrupt.

He hoped not again.

'So how was your day?' he said as his daughter slumped on the sofa. He logged out of the bank account, not being able to magic up any extra cash.

'Boring,' she said, looking up at the ceiling.

Mia was in her school uniform: navy blue trousers, white shirt and sensible black shoes with an inch of heel. Her jumper was stuffed in her book bag.

'Your mum says you've a cello exam tomorrow.'

'I'm sick of the cello,' she said with a grimace. 'All arpeggios and scales. And boring classical pieces.' She sat up in eagerness. 'How about we go out tonight with the tele-scope on the Flats?'

'Can't,' he said, closing the laptop. 'We're going to see a mate of mine from work. He plays jazz piano.'

'Is he any good?'

'Says he's got grade 4.'

'That's my exam tomorrow. Yuck.' She looked about her. 'I'm hungry. Got any decent food in or is it just the usual scraps?'

'I've shopped,' he said, unwilling to exchange insults with a teenager. 'He says bring your cello.'

'Cellos are not a jazz instrument,' she said adamantly. 'They're orchestral. That's the problem.' She sighed heavily as if the world's problems had been dumped on her shoulders. 'Violins can play jazz. Mum's got some music by Nigel Kennedy boogying along. And there's Stéphane Grappelli... Heard of him?'

'No.'

'Should've done. He played in the Hot Club de France.'

'How come you know this?'

'My music teacher played a piece by him the other day. He played with Django Reinhardt. Heard of him?'

'Didn't he have a finger missing or something?'

'Yeh. He was a gipsy. Amazing guitarist. Grappelli played with Yehudi Menuhin too. You must have heard of him.'

'Wasn't he a sprinter? Won the 400 metres in Beijing.'

'I don't believe I heard that.' She sighed with put on weariness. 'He was a famous classical violinist but also played jazz with Grappelli. Which brings me back to the cello. Double basses play in jazz quartets. But cellos? Never, ever heard of jazz cello.' She shrugged with finality. 'Besides, I can't improvise.'

'Ben may have some music,' he ventured.

'It won't be for a cello. How can it be? He's a pianist.' She'd dismissed the subject. 'I'm hungry.'

She rose and went into the kitchen.

This could be a tough evening, he thought. A reluctant cellist and a miserable pianist. Double tears on toast.

Chapter 9

Ben lived in a small house on Pevensey Road. They could have walked but Jack wanted to ease his daughter's pain, so they drove in the van, the cello in the back. It was in its soft case, only marginally protected from the ironware so Jack had enfolded it in the blanket he carried for wrapping his telescope when he went out stargazing.

They'd had a meal of baked potatoes, burgers and salad before they left, which satisfied Mia. Her mother, Alison, was a good cook. Amazing what she could knock up in no time, her job as head teacher forced her to be efficient. She refused to sink to junk food. Jack had added the salad as if Alison was looking down in judgement. Which in effect she was. No doubt she'd ask Mia what she had to eat at her Dad's.

While he'd been cooking, Mia had done some homework. Alison might have helped out, but Jack's knowledge of Spanish was limited to *una cerveza, por favor* which was useless to Mia, and to him as he no longer drank beer.

Ben invited them in. His hallway was crowded with a double extension ladder along the length on the floor stretching to the stairs, and with stacked up trestles. They had to squeeze by, with Jack holding the cello high over the obstructions. They went into a small sitting room.

The room had a dusty, stuffy smell as if the windows were never opened. There was a sunken green sofa, a desk overflowing with paperwork with mostly building supplies headings. How could he keep on top of the bills, Jack thought. But it wasn't his problem. A large flat screen TV had a grubby blue cloth over it, as if to keep it asleep like a budgerigar. A second armchair matching the sofa was full of boxes of tiles, as if keeping them comfortable. Tucked in amongst the papers was a saxophone with papers sticking out of the horn. But in pride of place was the keyboard on a stand with a chair in front.

Ben had showered; he was in a white shirt, the sleeves rolled up, and crumpled grey trousers.

'I've been limbering up,' he said to Mia. 'I hope you're not too good.'

'You've nothing to worry about,' she said.

She and Jack had hardly spoken on the way over. Seeing it from her point of view, Jack could see it might not be a lot of fun for a thirteen year old. Ben was around three times her age.

'I need a chair,' she said imperiously. 'Wooden. Not plastic.'

'Right-o,' said Ben. 'I like someone who knows what they want. Won't be a sec.'

And he left the room.

Mia unzipped the cello case.

'This is going to be hopeless,' she mumbled.

'We won't stay long,' said Jack in a hushed voice. 'He's my boss, and I want to get more work out of him. So do me a favour. Try to be nice.'

'Oh great! I'm your performing monkey. That's good to know.'

'It's not like that.'

'If I play well,' she said, digging the bow at him, 'can I have twenty quid?'

'That's cutting to the chase!' he exclaimed.

'Well?'

'Ten.'

'Fifteen.'

'OK, OK, but I want no messing about or sulking. And don't tell your mum.'

'What d'you think I am? Stupid?'

She had opened a small red tin which contained rosin. She took out the flat piece and gently waxed the fibres of the bow. It pleased him to see. His own musical education had been zero, he wished he'd learnt an instrument as a kid. Time gone, time wasted. Sure, there were some bad teachers, but some good ones too. He'd just taken against school, messed about and bunked off. Like a badge of honour.

At sixteen he knew everything. Or all he needed to know. But Alison showed him his ignorance. She took him around museums and gradually opened his eyes. Now his daughter was showing him up with classical music and jazz. He really should take an evening class.

Alison was right, keeping Mia to her practice. Kids being kids, they don't know what they want, he certainly hadn't. Don't always give in to them, Alison would say.

Easy to say, harder to act on with a complaining teenager.

Ben returned with a tray on which were a teapot, three mugs, small plates, walnut cake and a knife.

Jack noted the teapot and tray were grease splattered. Though the crockery was at least clean. He couldn't really complain, seeing how low he could fall. But he had no wish to see the kitchen.

'While the tea brews,' said Ben, 'let's play something.'

'I'm not good at improvising,' she said stiffly.

Here we go, thought Jack. They were an unlikely duo, he had to admit. Perhaps he should have protested homework to Ben. Or the music exam tomorrow. All his own fault, his eagerness to get more work.

'Just have a go,' said Ben. 'This is not the Albert Hall. No audience to ask for their money back.'

Except me, thought Jack, thinking of the fifteen quid Mia had finessed.

'Do you know *When the Saints Go Marching In?*' he said.

'Oh, that's easy. Let me have a go.'

She settled on the chair, the cello between her legs, and drew the bow across the strings. And winced a little at the note. 'Could do with a tune up.' And twisted the wooden screws, then played the note again. 'That'll do.' Haltingly, she began the tune. Way too slow, thought Jack. Then again, this time faster, and Ben tried to follow on the keyboard. Third time round she was playing half confidently, Ben trying to catch up. Even with Jack's musical knowledge close to zero, he realised Ben wasn't much good. Some of his notes were piercing.

They did another march round with the saints. Mia slowed to Ben's pace. It was something of a dirge. Jack gritted his teeth. It needed speed, it needed bounce. But Ben thumped like an elephant on the keys.

Taking her bow off the strings, Mia exclaimed, 'Your solo. Then me.'

Ben attempted to vamp around the well known tune. He was poor, hitting the keys with no variation, losing the tune. Mia caught Jack's attention and rolled her eyes. She was saying what he'd gathered himself, Ben wasn't much good. Jack was stuck being the audience, with nothing else to do. He couldn't watch TV or read a paper. He surreptitiously glanced at his watch. How much of this did he have to endure?

At last, Ben finished.

'Great!' shouted Jack, hating himself for sucking up to his boss.

'Take it away, girl!'

Mia took her turn, at first sticking to the tune, then going a little off it, and down a side track. She was better than Ben, but Jack could see from her face that she was struggling to improvise. Too halting, with too many off notes. She returned to the basic tune with relief. And Ben joined in somewhat mechanically. Ben was laughing, Mia straining not to run ahead of him.

Mia stopped, and Ben stopped.

'That was fun!' he exclaimed. 'You've earned tea and cake.' He turned to Jack. 'Best time I've had in a month. I hope you're proud of your daughter.'

Jack smiled, a smile born of tension eased, and relief the cacophony had stopped.

'I am,' he said.

Chapter 10

Mia and Jack went home at nine o'clock. Ben was in a good mood when they left, Mia had come out of her shell and was putting on a good show. She had done her best not to show him up, and kept at his pace. Following *When the Saints*, they had a go at a couple of nursery rhymes. *London Bridge is Falling Down* was followed by *Frère Jacques,* which Jack found no improvement. And had to stop looking at his watch. He'd tried to think about Heidi coming over tomorrow, about what he was going to do with his enforced leisure, but the discordant sounds broke in.

The US had used music as torture at Guantanamo Bay, and Jack could see how it would work. How it could break into any thought, force its attention on you until it was unbearable. He'd gone to the toilet when he didn't need to. And wished he hadn't. The toilet bowl was encrusted.

At last, he'd broken in and said Mia must get to bed as she had an exam tomorrow. So they did a last run around of *The Drunken Sailor* which Jack thought he couldn't play much worse.

But at least Ben was happy.

On the drive home, Mia said, 'He's never grade 4.'

'Where would you put him?'

'A grade 2 at a scrape. He's got no sense of rhythm.'

'He thinks he has.'

'Someone needs to tell him.'

Jack laughed. 'It's not going to be me.'

'I'm not going again. No way. I was awful, but listening to him hurt.'

'No help with tomorrow's exam then?'

She frowned at the reminder. 'None at all. I'll do some scales before bed.'

That surprised him. He hadn't had to ask.

Jack parked on their road, Earlham Grove. About to get out, she put her hand out, palm up.

'You owe me fifteen quid.'

'I'm a bit short at the moment,' he said uncomfortably.

'How much you got?'

'I'll give you a fiver for now.'

He took his wallet out of his back pocket and opened it. There were two fivers in it. Reluctantly he took one out and handed it to her.

'Is that all you've got?'

'I haven't been paid yet.'

'Give me it when you're paid.' She handed the banknote back.

Gratefully, he put the money away. 'Don't worry,' he said. 'I won't forget.'

'I won't let you.'

They got out of the van, Mia collected the cello from the back, and he locked up. And wondered about his bribing of Mia. For his part it was an investment in more work. To do so, he'd imposed on her the visit to Ben, without consultation. It could have been awful. Musically, it was. But it had got Ben out of his gloomy mood. Which was the point of it. OK, he'd have to pay up, and fair enough as Mia had had to work hard, playing and pretending that Ben was better than he was.

She'd done what was needed.

From over the road, a man in a three quarter length coat was crossing towards them, his shadow long in the setting sun.

'Fayyad!' exclaimed Jack. 'What are you doing here?'

'Can I have a word, Jack?'

'Sure you can. Come up for a cup of tea. You remember Mia?'

'Yes, we've met,' said Mia.

'You've got a lot bigger,' said Fayyad.

Mia screwed up her nose. 'Everyone says that.'

They went in and up the stairs to the flat. Jack was glad he'd tidied up somewhat in the afternoon, when Fayyad and his colleagues had cut short his working day.

Mia set up to practise in the sitting room. Jack and Fayyad went into the kitchen. He closed the door. The sound of her playing would come through, but hopefully not be too annoying.

'She's got a music exam tomorrow,' he said. 'Needs the practice.'

'Must be better than my son with his violin. What a wail!'

Jack put the kettle on and got the teapot ready. He sat down at the kitchen table.

'So, Fayyad, nice to see you, but I'm sure there's a point to this visit.'

Fayyad had settled on a stool and unbuttoned his smart, dark grey coat. He hadn't loosened his tie. He had his standards.

'You were there at the Cromer Court flats this afternoon,' he said, 'so you know a body was found in flat 1.'

'That's all I know,' he said. 'Your boss shooed us off after that.'

'Sorry about that, Jack. But I can confirm it's murder. And we must keep people away from the crime scene so as not to contaminate any evidence,' said Fayyad. 'We are allowing residents through the hallway, but no one else. Not even their friends or relatives.'

'I get that,' said Jack. 'Even if I'm losing money.'

'Can't be helped.'

Jack couldn't argue. Murder had to be investigated.

'Who was the victim?' he said.

'A mixed race guy, stabbed. The name of Kennedy Gerrard. Mean anything to you?'

'Never heard of him,' said Jack. 'How did you know he was dead? I mean, before you broke in.'

'We got an anonymous tip-off. You never know with those things. Can be someone playing a joke for whatever reason, but the man was pretty excited. So we reckoned there was a good chance it was genuine.'

Jack was thinking of his work that morning. All the time hammering and sawing outside a flat with a murdered man inside.

'I got to work about eight thirty,' he said. 'Didn't see anyone go into flat 1 all morning. Though I doubt the killer would use the front door. Not when we were there, at least.'

'Time of death is estimated to be in the early hours, one, maybe two o'clock. And your point, about the killer's access, is one we are looking at.'

The kettle had finished boiling. Jack poured the water into the pot and stirred. He took two clean cups off their hooks. It made a change not to have to wash them for a guest, though he doubted it would become a habit.

'So what do you want from me?'

Scales were playing in the other room. The cello was penetrating. Not too waily, he thought, just somewhat boring. To hear, as well as play.

'Our crime scene people will be there all day tomorrow,' said Fayyad. 'The day after, they'll restrict themselves to flat 1. You can have the hall again.'

'So just tomorrow off. That's good news. I can earn money again. I shall phone Ben. He's the gaffer on the job. That'll please him.'

Jack knew that Fayyad hadn't come to give him CSI's timetable. Not waiting outside just for that. Fayyad had a family in Ilford and would have been eager to be home. Jack had been invited round last summer. They had eaten out in the garden, the finest curry he'd ever had. With a mango/guava drink, no alcohol as they were Muslim. He recalled a pleasant evening as the sun set, long shadows down the garden.

'You'll be back working the day after tomorrow,' said Fayyad. 'So, Jack, we'd like you to keep your ears and eyes open.'

'Now we get to it,' said Jack. 'You want me to be your snoop.'

'I wouldn't use that term. A bit of help, let's say. It's murder, after all.' Jack sucked his lower lip as Fayyad went on. 'This afternoon, we did a little questioning of the people in the other flats. And got the impression they were afraid of Kennedy Gerrard. No one wanted to say much.'

Fayyad was a charmer, with his handsome, dark brown face, alert eyes and soft manner. Genuine though, he'd had lots of friends at school, being good at sport was a plus. Hard to turn him down. And it was a great curry.

'Put me in the picture on Gerrard,' he said.

'We've contacted the Council,' said Fayyad, 'It's not his flat. But according to the other residents, he's been living there a year.'

Jack was thinking about Heidi and her dodgy sublet.

'So how did he get the flat?' he said.

'The actual tenant is a disabled man, Amir Noor. We've tracked him back to his parents in East Ham. Hayley went to see him, and he told her that Kennedy Gerrard had beaten him up, smashed his gear, and in short terrorised him out of the place. And then Gerrard took over.'

'Nice guy.'

'We need to learn more about Gerrard. What the neighbours won't tell us. He may well have a police record, but it's likely he was living under an assumed name. Sure, we'll go through the contents of the flat, fingerprints, DNA, but there's always things people won't tell us. And seeing you are there...'

Jack poured out the tea and handed a mug to Fayyad.

'Me and the boss agree,' went on Fayyad. 'You're sharp, Jack. You've helped us out before.'

Jack smiled at the obvious flattery. It was working though, softening him up.

'Could his killing be drug related?' he mused.

'What led you up that road?'

Fayyad's eyes were fixed on him, alert to the question and Jack's response.

'I found a tin,' he said awkwardly. 'Under some ash, where the under-stairs cupboard was. It's got something in it. Could be drugs.'

'Where is it now?'

'In my van.'

Fayyad threw his hands up. 'You're telling me you've got a tin of drugs in your van?'

'I just said it could be drugs. Not definitely is.'

'Suppose it is,' went on Fayyad. 'If you got stopped, how would you explain it?'

'I'd tell the truth.'

'What? Say you found it and were going to hand it in.'

'Yes.' Knowing it sounded feeble even as he said it.

'Everyone says that, Jack.' He imitated a pleading voice. 'It's not mine, officer. Honest. I was going to hand it in, yackety yack.'

'But I have handed it in,' said Jack. 'To you. More or less.'

'Would you have done if I hadn't come round?'

'I was going to take it to the police station tomorrow.'

'Maybe you were, and maybe you weren't.' He held up a hand to stop Jack's response. 'We are a suspicious bunch, Jack. We've heard every lie under the sun.'

'Some people do tell the truth.'

'OK, OK.' Fayyad's hand went to his cheek. He thought for a second. 'You must say you gave it to me unprompted.'

'But I did.'

Fayyad smiled. 'Some would argue against that. But I'll go with it. Give me the tin when I leave.'

'Might not be drugs, though,' said Jack, protecting himself from his laxity.

An off-key note from next door made him wince. It was repeated, and then corrected.

'We'll have it analysed, Jack. Though you'd best come into the station tomorrow afternoon and we'll take a statement about how you found it.'

Jack knew to be careful. He should've handed in the tin straight away. But he hadn't. Neither had he mentioned Sol, the youngster he'd found surely looking for it. He wasn't a complete snoop. If he was going to be ears and eyes, it would be in his own way.

'So I'm off the hook?' he said.

'You offered me the tin unprompted. I shall say that with a clear conscience. And then you suggested you might assist us when you got back to work. Like the model citizen you are.'

Jack couldn't help a smile. Fayyad was no fool.

Chapter 11

As he wasn't working, Jack gave Mia a lift to school. On parting, he wished her luck with the exam. She'd practised first thing, waking him up before his alarm went off. Obviously anxious. He wondered about that as he made breakfast, the old standby, beans on toast. Who do you take exams for? For parents, for teachers, for other kids. Where do *you* come into it? All those scales, all that repetition. Does it teach you music?

Must do to some extent. She was playing a lot better than Ben last night. And wouldn't be without all that boring practice. And exams.

He'd only taken a few exams at school. Bunking off, not caring, teenage rebellion really. Stuff parents and teachers; the future didn't exist. Life was to be enjoyed. He lied to his parents. He knew best. He was the star in his own movie and it would all work out fine.

The comeuppance came when he left school. And all he could get were dead end jobs, hard graft and poor wages. At eighteen he was loading tiles, backbreaking work, alongside a man forty years older. The man was ordering him about, saying things which Jack knew were nonsense, but Jack was bottom of the heap and so had to listen to his ramblings.

He knew, if he didn't change, that old windbag would be him in forty years.

No qualifications didn't leave him many options, so he'd got into building, labouring at first. And took carpentry classes in the evenings. Hard after a day's work, but he was young and could handle it. After a year, he'd got his first job as a carpenter on a site. Luckily he was working with an older, experienced carpenter who taught him a lot, caught him before he went wrong, showed him the ropes and stopped the foreman sacking him. The two of them went on to the next job together. He hadn't seen Fred for fifteen years. Jack owed him a lot, and hoped he was OK.

Back home, around 9 am, he phoned Ben.

'Hello, Jack. You'd best be quick as I've got to go to court. We're trying to get bail for Tony.'

'Just one minute,' he said. 'Good news. My mate's a copper. That Asian guy, I was at school with. He says we can go back to work tomorrow.'

'Thank heavens for that. You never know with cops. They can shilly shally to their hearts' content. They don't care how much money I'm losing. Anyway, thanks for letting me know, Jack. It's a relief, just one day lost. And if the solicitor can get Tony bail there'll be three of us at work.'

Jack was unsure of Tony, who he reckoned was more trouble than he was worth. But no point saying that to a stressed dad.

'See you tomorrow, Ben.'

'Thanks for phoning, Jack. Really enjoyed last night. Cheered me up no end. Gotta go.'

Call done with, Jack made a cup of tea. It was a go-slow day, no timetable. Though he should make one or waste the day. He looked outside. It was pouring down, coming out of nowhere. He'd only been back fifteen minutes from dropping Mia off when it had been fine. Now the rain was shafting down, puddles filling in the gutters, volleys of droplets splashing onto car roofs and the road.

If he'd had work today, they'd be protected inside, but would be drenched filling the skip. So if it's going to rain, let it be today. And pray for clear skies tomorrow.

But what to do with a day off? There was always accounts, but not two days running. He knew how much he owed. He should get some leaflets printed. But you need money for that. All he had was two five pound notes. And Heidi was coming over for dinner tonight. Or was she? It had almost been fixed up. He'd meant to confirm it with her, then the cops came.

He looked out the window again, as if there might be a solution out there. Money falling from the heavens and not rain. He had another cup of tea. When in doubt have a cuppa, as his mother would say. A simple philosophy but tea did no harm.

He picked up his astronomy mag. Might clear up tomorrow. What's to see in June? Jack's prize possession was his telescope. When the night was clear, he'd go out onto Wanstead Flats to stargaze. Mia would often come. Midsummer wasn't the best of times, with the days too long; the sun hardly setting before it was up again. Though there was always the moon and the planets, but that was late in the evening. The magazine informed him, Jupiter was in the west about 10.30 pm, and Saturn getting to its zenith around midnight.

His phone rang. Not a number he knew.

'Hello, Jack of All Trades,' he said hopefully.

'My gutter's come off,' wailed a female voice. 'Water is pouring down my walls and coming through the air vent.'

'Plastic guttering?' he said.

'Yes. Can you come round?'

'Yes. You're in luck, I've got the day free because of an accident on site.' He wouldn't say murder as that invited too many questions.

'Serious accident?'

'Not too serious,' he lied. 'I'll be back to work tomorrow. Let's have your details and I'll be round as soon as the rain stops.'

He took down the address, and closed the call. He glanced out of the window. Still raining. Too bad. It mattered now; he couldn't work up a ladder in this. But he could prepare himself. He'd need his double extension ladder from his lock-up.

Chapter 12

The sawn-through padlock was on the ground at his feet. Each time he had opened up in the last few weeks he'd resolved to get a hardened steel one for the shutter, but there was always something more pressing. Besides, who'd bother to break in?

Someone had now. And nobody's fault but his own.

He looked at the mess inside the lock-up. It would never have won a prize for tidiness but today demonstrated how much worse it could be. A smashed bathroom sink, a paint can flowing through the scattered timber and broken glass. He poked a finger into the crust of white paint. It was still wet beneath. If he had a mind, he could calculate from the thickness of the skin when it had been spilt, and so estimate when the lock-up had been broken into.

And do what with the information?

He was wondering what to do first. He must secure the shutter but he had a job to get to. A space at the back glared from the whitewashed brickwork.

The vacant hooks should have held a double extension ladder.

That was the reason he'd come. To get the ladder, to do the gutter job. He'd told the woman he'd be there as soon as the rain had stopped. Not without a ladder, he wouldn't. Could he hire one? Of course, anything was hireable but he'd have to do some running around. And phoning.

All he had was ten quid.

He snapped his fingers. Ben had one. He'd seen it in the hallway of his house last night. Could hardly get through with the cello for ladders and whatnot. Ben wasn't using it, so no harm in asking.

He phoned.

'Hello, Jack. What can I do for you?'

'My double extension ladder has been stolen,' he said. 'I'm at my lock up, it's been broken into. And the ladder's gone. I've a guttering job to do right now. Can I borrow your ladder?'

'You can. But you'll have to come to Stratford Magistrate's court to get my keys. In the next ten minutes or so, I'll be in court for the bail hearing.'

'See you soon.'

Jack pulled down the locker. The mess would have to stay a while. He had a lock in his van, a cheesy thing that any hacksaw could get through, but better than nothing.

In less than a minute, he was in the van and driving away from Hampton Road, the lock-up being just down from the high street, in a short cul-de-sac where there were four garages, one of which was his. Convenient, walking distance from home or a one minute drive.

And should be locked properly.

Was there anything else missing? When the job was done, he'd check. Fortunately, his drills were OK. They were in a safe in the corner on the floor, weighing a ton. Bob had given it to him from a demolition job. It had taken four of them to get it off the truck and into the corner from where it was never ever going to be moved. In it, Jack kept various drills, a block & tackle, wrenches, his most valuable items apart from the ladder.

Jack was insured but any losses would be below the excess on the policy. Unless he cared to exaggerate them which wasn't worth the effort as they would only up his policy next year. In the insurance company v small builder arms race, the insurers always stayed ahead.

He drove down Earlham Grove, past his house, wind-screen wipers ensuring sight of the road humps and plane trees on either side. The rain had slowed, the full canopied trees swishing in the gusts. This was the quiet route, the main Romford Road would be too busy at the tail end of the rush hour.

Jack was thinking ahead. Where to park? All he needed was five minutes. Stratford shopping centre was too costly for no time at all. Morrison's supermarket. Though you needed to shop as you had to show your receipt to leave the car park.

Not in his version.

Getting into Morrison's car park was routine; the barrier lifted for him. It wasn't crowded and he parked. Jack leapt out his van and ran. It was raining lightly, the clouds light-ening. On the other side of the road was St John's church. In the churchyard, a man was sitting up in a sleeping bag, he must be soaked to the skin. With a hangover too. That was the way to get through a wet night, as Jack knew from his weeks on the streets. Booze away the cold and rain, and tomorrow's pain.

Past West Ham Lane and the old Town Hall where there'd been a fire twenty years ago. On his right was the obelisk in the middle of the road, must be 30 feet high, granite. He'd looked once to see who it commemorated. Gurney someone, no one he'd ever heard of.

A bus came close, through a puddle and splashing him in dirty water. He stopped a second, but nothing he could do about the wetness except curse Transport for London. Past what had been the *Two Puddings*, a dance dive of his youth. There used to be so many pubs in Stratford. The one ahead had been Bobby Moore's pub, the West Ham hero, England captain of the World Cup winning team of '66.

He scampered up the steps of the Magistrates Court, brushed himself down before going in the wide doors, into the hushed marble foyer. Which court? There were people milling, many in suits, some in black gowns, the costly barristers. The suits might be solicitors or criminals; you couldn't always tell them apart. Ah, there was Ben on a bench. In a suit too, twisting his neck in the stiff collar and tie.

'Looking smart, Ben.'

'Have to be,' he said. 'Might have to speak up for Tony.' He looked Jack up and down. 'You're soaked.'

'A bus splashed me. But I'm not appearing in court. Got the keys for the ladder?'

Ben fished them out of his pocket. 'These are Tony's. Give 'em back to me tomorrow.'

Jack took the keys and shook Ben's hand gratefully.

'Cheers, Ben. I owe you one for this. But must go, if I'm to get the work. See you tomorrow.'

And he was away, clattering across the shiny floor, through the door and away from the world of gowns and suits, long windows, marble flooring and wood panelling. Would he get a fair hearing if he was pulled in by the scruff of his neck?

Or Tony for that matter. How many of them would be working on site tomorrow?

The rain had stopped. So the woman would be expecting him, looking out of her window, waiting. He'd best put her at ease. Jack phoned while he walked back to the car park. He told her he'd be there in twenty minutes. She couldn't see his wet overalls or know he didn't yet have a ladder.

In Morrison's car park, Jack figured what he had to do. He had to follow on the tail of another driver, so close that as the barrier lifted, he could get through too.

Jack drove from his parking space to ready himself, waiting near the turn for the exit barrier. Within a minute, a blue car came past him and Jack followed in its wake. The car got to the barrier, showed the receipt, the long arm lifted, the car drove through with Jack close behind, almost hitting the blue car in his haste. The barrier arm slapped down on his roof, scratching the edge as he came free of it.

He'd probably be banned, but that was a problem for another day.

Chapter 13

The work didn't take long. A couple of screws had come loose in a gutter bracket which should have been holding the guttering to the board below the roof. The gutter sagged and rainwater had poured off the roof, missed the gutter where the bracket was loose, and had run down the wall and into the air brick.

No fittings were broken which made life easier or he'd have to go off buying. Always a nuisance as you had to take the pieces along to the store to get exact replacements in order to fit with the rest of the guttering and downpipe. Each manufacturer had, of course, different seals and screwins so you couldn't use, say, one type of bend with another's gutter. On one job, the manufacturer had gone out of business, when all he needed was the piece from the gutter to the downpipe. What should have been a small job would have meant total replacement if he hadn't been able to buy the right bit of the defunct guttering on eBay.

This one was straightforward. All that was necessary was to remove a section of guttering, move the bracket along a few inches and put in new screws to secure it to the board. Then put the gutter back in, and all was done and dusted.

Luckily, Ben had had a stand-off in his hall as well as the ladder. Jack had one in his lock-up but in his rush to get to the court had forgotten to bring it. He knew well enough you never rest a ladder on guttering. A stand-off bolts to the top of a ladder, and rests against the wall just below the guttering, giving a support at the top. A builder he knew had broken his back when the guttering came down and the ladder slipped. He was now in a wheelchair living on benefits.

Working on his own, Jack knew he'd be a fool to take risks on ladders. Though he'd known plenty who did, mostly getting away with it. But one day, there would be the time when they wouldn't. You could bet on it. Window cleaners and builders, twenty feet in the air, with the weight of their ladder resting on thin plastic and a few screws, oblivious to hazard.

On another day, he would have charged the woman £50, but the thought of a new ladder he'd have to buy and a new lock for the lock-up caused him to up it to £75. She paid cash, he counted it, was tempted to give her twenty back, but hadn't he come quickly and gone to a lot of trouble to get the ladder?

Bella paid up without quibble. Jack wondered, what might another builder have charged her? Was he getting out of touch with pricing? He was reluctant to up his prices, but accidents happen, tools get damaged, stolen, the van needed too many repairs. Bella asked him to look at the inside wall in her sitting room where the water had come through the airbrick. He examined it and told her the wall needed to dry out before any work could be done on it. With luck, the wall would just need scraping, a bit of plaster work and repainting. If she was unlucky, the plaster would bubble up to such an extent that the whole wall would need re-plastering. Wait and see.

One for the future. Always good. He'd come back in two weeks. The best thing about building work: surprises. The worst thing too, considering the body in flat 1.

He left Bella. She was OK with the price, that's the main thing. And considering him for another job. All considered, it had worked out. First stop was getting the ladder and stand-off back to Ben's. Then to his lock-up to sort that out. Good to have 75 quid in his pocket. Not enough for a ladder but it would cover a decent lock for the lock-up, that had to be a priority, and the meal tonight with Heidi.

At Ben's place, he carried in the ladder and laid it along the hallway at floor level where it had been previously. He put the stand-off on a pile of boxes containing floor tiles, knocking off a Huntley & Palmer biscuit box. The tin lid came off as it hit the floor sprinkling out a rain of washers. Not drugs this time round, if the tin found under the stairs did have them in.

Jack reflected as he picked up washers from the floor. Why had he found the tin? And not Tony, who had been working under the stairs before he went on his ill-fated sortie to get them breakfast? Tony had been keen to go out, too keen perhaps. And gone to the betting office. But just maybe, he'd come home too.

Having put the washers back in the biscuit box, Jack looked up the stairs. The house was empty; Fayyad wanted him to snoop. So Jack went up. Father and son were in court, so no hassle.

On the steps, along the wall, were boxes of screws, rolls of electrical wiring, drill bits, remnants of past jobs. The landing was similarly littered. There was a ladder to the loft whose trap door was open, and Jack could make out timber and copper pipe. It was only a small house and Ben obviously used it as his store. There were three rooms up here. The bathroom with its toilet which he had visited when he'd come with Mia for the music session last night. And two other rooms. One would be Tony's room, the other Ben's.

He tried a door. It was an untidy bedroom, the bed unmade, the sheets grey. Underwear and clothing on the floor told him it was Tony's room. What exactly was he looking for?

Suppose Tony had found something on site, under the stairs. He'd need to get it away, so he volunteered to get their breakfast. But first, he'd come home to offload it. Might have gone to the café first, ordered the takeaway breakfast, told them he'd be back in ten minutes.

If so, he could have hidden something here. But quickly, as he had to be back to collect breakfast and be back on site. The betting office escapade didn't quite fit, except maybe it did, as gamblers lose their logic pretty quickly. Just suppose he came home. Stay with that. Where would you shove something in a hurry?

Jack lifted the mattress. And there was a tin box, in the schoolkid hiding place, almost identical to the one he'd given Fayyad, the remaining paint peeling. The lid was still jammed on which suggested Tony knew what was in it. Jack thought of taking it away, but then he'd be the obvious suspect as Ben had given him the keys.

He photographed it with his phone, putting it on the mantelpiece by the clock with a photo of a teenage Tony and a woman, who he judged to be his mother. That would show the room where it had been.

A door opened downstairs. Heavens! must be Ben back. He could hear voices, the two of them. Jack shoved the box under the mattress. And quietly left the room, closing the door after him. Someone was coming up the stairs. Jack at once was in the bathroom. He locked the door.

Jack sat on the edge of the bath. And recouped his breath, hoping he hadn't been seen coming out of Tony's room.

The door was shaken.

'Who's in there?' It was Tony.

'Me, Jack,' he called, 'having a dump. Won't be a minute.'

'What you doing here?'

'I brought the ladder back. And got caught short.'

'Right. Hurry up. I'm dying.'

Jack counted fifteen. He couldn't come straight out.

'Come on, come on, I'm about to burst!'

'I'm done,' he called and pulled the toilet handle to flush. He played out a few seconds as if to adjust his clothes. Then turned on the tap and washed his hands. Might as well make them look clean. He wiped them on the grubby towel. And opened the door.

'I needed that.'

Tony, outside, was jumpy. 'Let me get in there. Dad's making tea. See you downstairs.'

He went in the bathroom, closing the door. Jack went down the stairs, relieved he'd been sharp when he'd heard the front door open. Tony didn't seem suspicious, so he must act normal. He'd brought back the ladder and needed the toilet. That's all.

Stick to it.

Ben was in the kitchen, the back room of the house. It made Jack's own seem the epitome of tidiness. Dishes were piled high in the sink, dirty pots on the draining board and on the stove. More cardboard boxes were piled around, of tiles, of plumbing fittings. The floor was scuffed and almost black.

Cleanliness was relative. Jack did a cursory clear up every time Mia came over. And a fuller one when Alison was due. His efforts certainly stopped the pile up that this room illustrated. They had no reason to clear up. Just two messy builders coming and going. It was clear too, they barely noticed, whereas Jack had some guilt whenever he had visitors.

'I see you brought the ladder back,' said Ben, incongruous in the untidy kitchen in his smart suit and tie.

'Thanks,' said Jack. 'Got me a bit of cash in hand. Had to use your stand-off too.'

'No problem. Staying for a cup of tea?'

Obviously he was, though Alison would have turned her nose up in disgust and walked out. If she was his standard boiling point, this would be his at any other time. Though a cup of tea in a less than clean cup with his boss wouldn't kill him. Or he'd be dead fifty times over.

'Yeh, thanks.' There were only two chairs, how was this going to work out?

'Sit down,' said Ben. 'We got bail for Tony. So three of us tomorrow.'

'That's good,' he said. 'Get a move on with the work.'

'Do you want some toast?'

Jack looked at the pile of dishes and wondered how plates would be salvaged to put the toast on, or a knife to butter the bread, as the heap almost touched the taps, allowing no room to wash anything.

'Just tea,' he said. 'The client gave me some grub.'

Tea was hot and killed bugs, cooling toast collected them. Tony joined them, both utterly besuited, as if back from a family wedding. Tony took the other chair and tore off his tie.

'Thank God that's over,' he said. 'I thought I was going to be banged up till the trial.'

'You can't go around hitting people,' said his father putting bread into an almost hidden toaster.

'Don't lecture me, Dad,' said Tony wearily. 'I got it the first time.'

'It costs,' exclaimed his father, shaking a knife at him. 'Lawyers don't work for nothing.'

'I'll pay you back.'

'What with?'

'I got money coming.'

'From where?'

'From you. I'll be working tomorrow. And I got a few angles of my own I'm working on.'

'Like what?'

Tony threw up his hands. 'Leave me alone, Dad. I've had the cops on my back. Now you. I'm allowed some privacy.'

He turned to Jack. 'See what he's like? I tell you this, never work for your old man. It's lecture, lecture, lecture. Nothing is secret.'

Ben was somehow washing a plate in cold water in the minute space between the dirty dishes and the tap. Jack wondered how he'd fit in a cup, keeping well out of this family spat.

'I give you a job, I pay for your lawyers,' exclaimed Ben turning off the tap. 'I don't expect gratitude. When have I ever had that? If your Mum was here...'

'Don't bring her into it.'

'She wanted to be proud of you.'

Tony sighed with exasperation. 'She might yet be. I'm not dead, you know.'

There was silence as Ben washed cups with a filthy sponge, managing to get enough water inside them to give them a semblance of a rinse.

Tony sat back, his chair resting on two legs, feet on a cardboard box.

'Your mate's a copper,' he said to Jack.

'Yeh,' said Jack. 'He told me we could get back to work tomorrow.'

'Tell you anything else?'

'No. The rest, he said, is operational. He can't tell me anything.'

'Not even about the victim, who it is and whatever?'

'Nothing about him at all.'

'Oh, so it's a him then.'

Tony was sharp, Jack had best be careful. He had to pretend ignorance.

'He told me just that much. A bloke was dead in the flat. I don't know how he died. Heart attack, murder, I don't know.'

'They don't make it a crime scene for a heart attack. Got to be murder.'

'You're probably right,' said Jack. 'But he didn't say.'

But Fayyad had, of course. The man was stabbed, Kennedy someone, odd first name. Listening to Tony, and taking care with his replies, Jack hadn't seen Ben emptying the teapot. There certainly wasn't room to rinse it out with the pile of crockery in the sink. Still, Tony and Ben were healthy enough, so it seems we can take a fair amount of dirt. Though maybe they were immune to the house bugs which could well fell him.

Ben's face was stern as he buttered the toast. Tony plainly did his own thing and expected Dad to rescue him when it went wrong.

Jack said, 'If you don't mind me asking, why did you go to the betting office yesterday?'

'To put a bet on. Why do you think?'

'Just, they don't do bacon sandwiches.'

Tony swung his legs off the box, and leaned forward on the table.

'Two old geezers going at me.' He sighed, hard done by. 'I went in the café. Made me order, skipped down the betting office while they were getting it ready. Satisfied?'

'They don't arrest people for putting a bet on,' said Jack, knowing he was pushing it, but Tony's cockiness annoyed him.

Tony's eyes rolled. 'Change the subject. I've had more than enough of this.'

Ben put the plate of toast on the table. Then a pot of jam with a knife on top. Side plates were not included.

He said, 'The manager asked Tony to leave. There was a bit of a fracas, cops were passing. And it all got exaggerated. Depending who you talk to.' Ben added jam to the top slice of toast without removing it from the heap, until covered. 'The magistrate granted bail on the condition that he keeps away from that betting shop.'

'Which I will.' Tony repeated the actions of his father, working on the top slice on the pile. It was a neat routine, doing without secondary plates. 'And don't worry, I'll be in work tomorrow and do my share.'

Having seen how it worked between father and son, Jack wanted his tea, so he could drink up quickly and leave them to their row. The threesome was too uncomfortable to sit through much longer. Ben, he gathered, could have a go at Tony for his behaviour, but if anyone else did then he'd side with his son.

East End Dad, protecting the family. Harangue the teacher for having a go at your kid, then belt them when you got home. Jack made a mental note: lay off Tony, no matter what he does. Watch him, he has plenty to hide, and a temper, not good if you have secrets.

He'd more or less worked out what Tony had done yesterday when he'd gone off with the breakfast money. Taken the tin with him, gone home with it and hid it under the mattress. Presumably he couldn't slip two tins up his shirt, so concealed the other under rubble, not expecting to be arrested. He'd gone to the café to make the order, that was logical. Belted off home, where rationality flew out the window and Tony then went to the betting shop. Had he lost the money he and Ben had given him? Or gone there to see someone. No point asking him. And then he'd struck someone, pretty heftily, and the cops were called.

Pity the tea was so hot or he'd just swill it back and go.

'Do you think the Hammers will escape relegation this season?' he said.

Football, a safe topic. That's if father and son were West Ham supporters.

Chapter 14

Tony was lying flat out on his bed, shoes still on. His hands were behind his head on the grubby pillow. He'd left Jack and Ben at the kitchen table, had thought of sitting on the stairs and listening in. But rejected it. He knew what they'd be saying.

Jack had been in the house when they got back from court. Upstairs. Tony had heard a door bang, and so rushed upstairs and found Jack in the bathroom. Had he been in his bedroom? Tony had had a quick shifty after he'd been to the loo. The gear was still under the mattress, the lid still jammed on. Though the clock seemed closer to the photo of him and Mum.

Maybe he was just nervy.

He'd been surprised that Jack stayed on, with him and Dad bickering like an old married couple. Ben wants him to be grateful all the time. No way. You can't spend your whole life saying thank you. You end up like a weed with everyone robbing you and taking advantage. He talks about Mum like she was a saint. That's what happens when you're dead. You can do no wrong. All the time he says, what would your mother think. Blah, blah. She's three years gone and no angel. She'd clip him round the ear-hole until he got too big for it. Dead and buried, move on. You can't keep looking back: I should've done this, I should've done that. You didn't. And that's that.

Not so easy though, he had to admit. He shouldn't have gone for the manager. She's just a pawn, a wage slave. They big her up, call her manager, give her a uniform, say she is in charge, which is a laugh. They're pulling her strings, she sings and dances to their tune, total. She says, 'Out. You're banned from here.' Tony had just come in to tell the guys about the stuff he'd picked up. So he ignored the manager, trying to get the guys away from the TV race on the screen and angle his chat around to business when she was phoning the law. Tony snatched the phone off her, threw it across the shop and shook her up a bit. That's his side. A bit of annoyance.

She says he grabbed her by the throat, but you couldn't see that on the CCTV, too many people milling about. He shook her by the shoulders, that's what he's sticking to. Let 'em prove otherwise. Who trusts bookies anyway? They take your money, happy to do that all day long, tell you about all these novel bets where you can't go wrong. It's like new sweeties to tempt you when it's just sugar, and more sugar, all day long. Punters bet, punters lose, punters get mad. That's the way of the world. What do they expect when they are robbing you blind? All smiles and salaams.

He wasn't going back inside. No way. Should've sweet talked her, instead of thrashing out. Too easily wound up, but one lot of bird is enough. A waste of a life, all those rules and searches. Worse than school. Though he'd made a few contacts. That's all it was good for. Life on hold, treated like a total kid. The few pennies they give you, you spend on smokes and that's that. All gone. All the conniving, just to get a few coppers more, for another quarter ounce. Such small beer, such a tiddly world. It makes you small too. Kills your plans.

Make it big or don't bother. He was at his dad's, but he wasn't staying. Just a base.

There was that other box. He couldn't have got the two out. Not with Dad and Jack there. One he could shove down his trousers. The other he'd hid in the rubble.

Who got it?

The cops? Possible. Ben had said the cops had ordered them out. That guy killed in number 1. He knew it was Kennedy Gerrard. Knew he was dead. But you have to play dumb.

The other box. If not the cops, how about Jack? Ben had left him on his own. He could've found it, sussed what it was and snaffled it. Maybe that's what he was doing at their house, thinking there might be another. Sneaky bastard. He'd been asking Tony all those questions. Like what did he really want to know? Did he go into his bedroom?

Suppose he did. Suppose he found the box. It was hardly hidden, Tony hadn't had time. Suppose he's got the other one. What's he going to do with it? He hasn't got the contacts. Tony mulled this over. What if he has it and has his own ideas? A quiet word with Jack was due. Find out if he has it. Offer a deal, just to see whether or not. Though Jack wouldn't see a penny, not when Tony was done with him.

Chapter 15

Jack was relieved to leave the Wilson house. Tony had left them but Ben kept grousing, and Jack pleaded he had work to do. True enough, but he needed fresh air. Their kitchen was filthy and claustrophobic. He wondered whether Tony suspected him of having taken the tin from the site. Well, he'd got rid of it. The cops now had the tin. Whatever was in it.

Out of his hands.

But he'd moved items on the mantelpiece in Tony's bedroom for the photo he took. And hardly had time to put them back in place when the front door opened. Had he got away with it? A little displacement, is that the sort of thing you notice?

Jack doubted if Tony would. Or really, it's not the sort of thing you can be sure about. It's not enough by itself. Forget it, he told himself. The sun was shining after the earlier rain, a contrast to the gloomy house. Ben's wife had probably kept it clean and left her menfolk too dependent on her. The way Ben spoke of her, Jack reckoned she would not have allowed ladders and boxes in the hall and especially not in her kitchen. Her domain. But three years had passed, and, with no one to stop encroachment, the stuff built up, job by job. Crockery was grudgingly washed when needed. Neither of them knew which end of a mop was which.

He could talk.

And couldn't help a grin as he strolled up to the high street. Alison had a particular face when she sniffed around and complained at his neglect of his flat. Was this a male/

female thing? Men tolerating mess more? Though he'd known messy women, especially in his drinking days. Maybe it was men who were over-mothered, not expected to do housework. So they lived in squalor when without female aid.

He was hungry. It was early afternoon and he'd had a busy morning. Rushing here and there to get the ladder, doing the gutter job, getting the gear back to Ben's and then refusing toast in the filthy kitchen. But on the bright side, seventy five quid, cash in hand from the job. A bit of luck there, with the cops preventing work on site, the small job would just tide him over.

And then he recalled the stolen ladder. That would have to be replaced. When? With what? He must tidy the lock-up. The Wilson household had woken his awareness. Do it while he had time, before he shrugged it off. An hour there, then eat.

The traffic was busy on Woodgrange, busier now they had widened the pavement at the expense of the road. Slow, coughing traffic on either side, the pavements busy. He'd read there were only 15% British whites in Forest Gate. And been surprised, as mostly he didn't notice, people being people and the tendency to keep with your own. Gazing down the road, he was struck by the variety: men in traditional Asian dress, women with burqas pushing pushchairs, a smattering of whites, a few black people. A multi-racial area, as they say. It didn't do to keep counting. Just people. What would you do with the numbers anyway?

Everyone's got to live, that's all he knew.

In his time, he'd done jobs for whites, Muslims, Hindus, Sikhs, blacks. All customers. Any one of them could give you grief, or a cup of tea and biscuits.

The lock-up was still secure, though the cheap lock on the hasp accused him. So tidy up, have some grub, buy a decent lock. That would do for the day. Was tonight the meal with Heidi? His place, but she didn't have his address.

It wasn't happening. Forget it. Damn the cops. But they'd go. It was only a small flat they were in. And then he'd see her again. He always ran too quickly. He didn't know her, she didn't know him. Too easy to fantasise when you know next to nothing about someone. She can be the dream until you are arguing over a film, politics, about being dragged over the Flats with his telescope. That woman, what was her name? She'd said, he had forced her to go. He had denied it. She'd yelled, how could she refuse when she didn't know. It was two hours of cold boredom.

What was her name?

But seventy five quid in his pocket, almost made up for the ladder going. And maybe Heidi some time. Close the curtains on further thoughts.

Jack undid the temporary lock, tempted to throw it away but he'd need it for a while, and lifted the shutter. Nothing had changed; no lock-up fairy had raced around to bloom the garage in Disney sparkle. How to begin? He was tempted to pull down the shutter and walk away. It was a disheartening wreck. There was no money to be made in tidying up. He stopped himself, that was the Wilson attitude. Not exactly a good example. He was here, he'd get going. A general tidy then.

He must make space at the front for the broken toilet and sink, for general rubbish that had to be taken to the dump at Jenkins Lane. That would be an hour's journey, driving down, disposing of it, and driving back. Somehow, he'd fit it in after lunch, along with buying a lock.

In a corner were some thick plastic bags, he took one and began filling it with broken glass, smashed bathroom tiles, bits of wood which might have done for something someday but hadn't yet, so might as well go in the bag. His long spirit level! He'd been searching for it a few weeks back when he had to repair a wall. In the end, he'd bought another for ten quid as he couldn't work without it.

Which proved clearing up wasn't a total waste of money. Just there were limits. And there lay the nub of the argument between him and Alison, between him and the Wilsons. Except he had no intention of challenging his boss. He didn't have to live in their mess. And Ben had lent him a ladder.

The stand-off was here too. And in the course of the stacking, binning and rearranging, he found two chisels, a claw hammer and a telescope light filter. How on earth had that got here? Probably when he'd brought in dust sheets from the van.

It was so inefficient. This never ending tidying up. He'd read a few months back about entropy in his astronomy magazine. Disorder, mess, in the universe. He couldn't get his head round it, and looked it up on Wikipedia. Whenever you do anything, you create a mess. It applies to every process in the universe. It's why there can't be a hundred per cent efficient machine, or perpetual motion which comes to the same thing. Mess making is wasted energy.

He'd been almost overwhelmed when he'd first read about it. A new way of seeing everything. The connections between big and small. Entropy sounded better than mess. More scientific. And found it everywhere he looked. Litter on the streets, at home of course, on the tables of cafés, the gunk building up on his sparking plugs, the dirty decorating sheets which he really must clean.

Sweep, wash, hoover.

So much wasted time and energy tidying up by everyone, even the Wilsons who did the minimum. But he had to admit the lock-up did look better, with the added bonus of the tools he'd found, which he put tidily in a toolbox. Face it; you can't do a job without making a mess. It cannot be done. So simple, and yet he'd never connected.

It blew his mind, how this lock-up related to a fundamental law of the universe.

After three quarters of an hour, Jack had had enough. Universal law or not, he could only stand so much tidying. Though it did look more ordered, the entropy decreased. At the expense of his work. If he'd worked at school, he could've been a scientist.

Mess made work. So simple, so obvious. OK, the ladder brackets on the back wall glowered in their emptiness. Must get a ladder, but when would he have the hundred to spare?

A worry for another day.

There were four sacks full of broken oddments including stuff he'd kept for some time never, all in the corner by the open shutter, along with the smashed sink and toilet bowl. All in place, so he could come back with the van after lunch, load up and take them to Jenkins Lane dump, hand over his entropy to the Council, and on the way back, buy a lock.

It was all go. Good news, bad news. The cops in, but for only a day and a half, ladder stolen, but a cash in hand job. A dead body in flat 1 and a date tonight from flat 2.

And a tidy lock-up. He had a last glance round. Not bad at all. Timber stacked, tools all put away, a step-ladder on top of a wheelbarrow, decorating sheets folded and stacked. He'd made spare room too. That would go soon enough. Entropy trumped all suits.

Jack locked up. Even as he did so, he thought of going straight off and buying a proper lock. But he was too hungry. Time enough after lunch. And he headed out of the short cul-de-sac, relieved it was done, but pleased he'd stuck to it, and up Hampton Road to the high street. Across the road, through the slow traffic, was Forest Café. He could go home and make something, he had food in, but after his efforts this morning, he deserved a cooked lunch made by somebody else.

Waiting to cross the road at the lights, he saw Sol walking on the other side. The young black lad, a wiry body with dreadlocks, who'd been looking for the tin, or was it tins? He was walking quickly with a backpack, swerving in and out of other people on the pavement as if he had an assignation with destiny.

The lights changed and Jack crossed the road, and followed in his wake, utterly curious about where he was going in such a rush. Jack had to get a move on, or he'd lose him. Sol couldn't go faster without running. Other people were more leisurely, strolling or standing about, only he and Sol were in a hurry. Jack circled round street furniture, headed through the bus stop shelter and lost him.

He wasn't up ahead, Jack was pretty sure of that, weaving side to side to be sure. So he must have gone into a shop. Not Greggs the bakers, nor Woodgrange Household, though that was a deep shop, so maybe down the far end buying a mop. Not likely. You don't rush for that.

There he was, in AttaBet. Jack could see him through the glass door. Sol was at the gambling machines, in a row of four. Jack held back, but remained curious about the young man's hurry. Why shouldn't he go in himself? Anyone can place a bet. He pushed open the door and entered.

There were maybe ten people in the shop, all black apart from himself, most of them watching a large raised TV screen, where horses and jockeys were parading round a ring. They glanced at him, but he didn't feel hostility. He knew from experience, that different betting shops gathered up different clientele. This was mostly West Indian men, young to middle aged, to going on old.

Having come in, Jack knew he had to be a punter and picked up a racing paper. And made out to look through the runners and riders at a horse race meeting. After half a minute of perusal, he looked about him and could see the regulars had lost interest in him. By making out he was watching the TV screen, he could keep half an eye on Sol, who was only a little off his sight line. Maybe Sol had seen him, maybe he hadn't but there was no point trying to hide. He was just a builder putting on a bet; what was wrong with that?

Sol was concentrating on his machine. He had a bundle of screwed up notes in one hand. He would feed one in the machine, press the button and the machine did its stuff, Jack couldn't see what he was playing as the angle didn't allow it. Every twenty seconds or so, Sol took a note from the fistful and poked it in the machine. Jack pretended interest in the 1.30 at Haydock, taking in none of the burble about horses and the going, as his focus was the young man.

Sol slotted in the last note from his fist. He put his hand in the backpack in the stool by the side of him and pulled out another bundle of notes held together with an elastic band. Sol took off the band, shoved it in the backpack, and set to feeding the hungry machine.

'You watching the boy?' said a man by him.

Jack turned to the elderly, thickset black man, in a brown leather jacket. His face was weathered, hair short and grizzled. A West Indian accent, maybe Jamaican.

'I was watching the runners and riders,' said Jack, indicating the TV screen. 'And saw him feeding the machine. On and on.'

'He's one busy boy,' said the man with a grin. He had gaps in his teeth and a single gold one in the upper centre. 'He will put it all in. You see.'

'What's he playing?'

'Roulette.'

'How's he get all that cash?'

The man gave a closed-lipped grin and patted Jack on the shoulder. 'You too curious, man. Keep your nose out if you don't want to end belly up by the Woolwich Ferry.'

'I'm not much of a swimmer,' said Jack looking back at the screen. The horses were going into their places at the starting gate.

'They won't give you a rubber ring, them fellas.' He grinned. 'I tell you one thing. It makes me laugh when I t'ink about it.' He leaned in and said softly, 'He only bets on number two.'

'Nothing else?'

'Nothing else.'

Jack scratched his head. 'He's bound to lose. The odds are in the machine's favour.'

'2.7 per cent. But he comes up 97.3 per cent.'

Jack shook his head. This wasn't making sense.

The man chuckled. 'Him really got you puzzled.'

'I don't get it. He's putting it in as fast as he can. Where's his winnings?'

'He get a voucher when he cashes up. Take it to she.' He indicated the woman in the glass kiosk with his stubby pen. 'She put it in his bank account.'

It hit Jack, how it worked. Sol was taking a small loss to get the money into his account.

'Dodgy money to good money,' he said.

'Him can't take it to the bank, man.' He chuckled.

The race had started; the commentator attempting to keep up with the pack, that rapid, auctioneer like spiel, words galloping along with the mounts.

The man beside him was fixed on the screen.

'Stay with dem!' he yelled.

Jack knew as much as he was going to know, but how to get out of the betting office without looking suspicious?

He went to a fixed odds machine, one of a pair, some way from Sol. Lights were flashing around the big roulette wheel on the display. Jack was bewildered, it looked so complicated. He held a ten pound note at the slot for notes. Hesitated. Then thrust it in, and regretted it as the machine swallowed it.

All he could do was play. Jack limited himself to a pound a spin. All the lights and noise, he could see the way it could take hold. The roulette wheel was as big as a dart board, all colour and flash. Keep it simple, he told himself, or he'd be lost forever. He bet on black. Stay with lucky black. There were lots of other ways to bet, too many, but a bet on black required just one finger.

It was speedy. Twenty seconds for a single spin on the electronic wheel. In five minutes, he'd lost his ten but had won eight credits. This could easily get addictive. Get away, he told himself, the excitement making him sweat. All too easy. You win, you lose. There's always the chance of winning more. Go for bigger odds. Enough, he must get away before he was sucked in. Jack pressed a button, a slip of paper came out of the slot. He took it to the cashier and cashed in the eight credits.

With the eight pounds in his hand, he thought, why not? One more go on the machine. Get his money back. But someone had taken over his terminal and the other three in the shop were occupied too.

Get out of here.

Jack left the shop and walked rapidly down the street, relieved to have only lost two pounds. Away, away, spend money on food, not dropped into the bottomless pit of the bookie's pocket.

Chapter 16

Jack was in the Forest Café at a table midway down. The lunch rush was finishing, and he had a table to himself. Food at last, after all morning running around. He'd gone for the all day breakfast: chips and beans and sausages and eggs, with toast and a big mug of tea. Comfort food. Alison would turn her nose up at the lack of greenery. Heart Attack Special was her phrase.

He slowed up his eating, there was no rush. He had the debris in the van to cart away, he'd earned money this morning. Take it easy, the maxim of life. Taste what's going into your mouth. Someone had said that at Alcohol Halt. He couldn't remember who.

He wiped a broken egg with a piece of toast, took a bite and savoured the fat and protein, the good and bad of it. You can't worry about every bite. That's if every bite is the same bite, Alison would say. How had she sneaked into this conversation? Would she never leave his life? Not now, a phone call away, their joint daughter the tie between them.

Sometimes he would not think of her all day, other days he was arguing with her every other minute. OK, he said, as he carved a sausage, what was Sol up to, Alison? Alison had nothing to say on the subject, which was the point of asking. The young man had been pouring money into a machine, always betting on the same number, and so bound to lose but bound to win some. At the end he would come up with maybe 97% of what he'd put in, but it would be legal money that went into his account. But where did he get all that cash in the first place?

There weren't many possibilities. Either stolen or from drugs. Sol was laundering it.

Did that connect to Pandora's box? The one he'd handed over to Fayyad. Sol was looking for it in the dust and rubble, no doubt about that. But Jack had found one of them first and Tony another. But Sol had loads of cash. With a man dead in flat 1. Did that connect? A repellent man who had harassed a disabled man out of the flat and taken over.

Lots of broken threads like a vandalised junction box, but with no colour coding to tell which connected to which.

He was considering another cup of tea before heading off to the town dump, when Heidi came into the café. She was a little overdressed for a warm day, in greenish tweed skirt and jacket, half heels, and a crisp yellow blouse. She saw him, gave a little wave, and came over.

'Just in for a quick coffee,' she said.

Jack called to Faz at the counter. 'A coffee and a tea, mate.'

Faz gave a thumbs up. Heidi sat down. She took off her jacket and put it carefully on the back of the chair.

'You look like you're appearing in court,' he said.

'Not far off,' she said, blowing out her cheeks. 'Flat hunting. I'm going to traipse around estate agents. I hate it. Rubbishy flats to see, smarmy landlords, all too expensive. But got to live somewhere.'

'What's happened?'

'Cops. That's what's happened. Cromer Court is swarming with them. I was interviewed by that tall woman about the murder in flat 1.' She stopped for an instant. 'You do know it was a murder?'

He did, but wasn't going to show he was in the know.

'I guessed something was up with all those cops. Breaking the door in. Crime scene tape. They don't do that for natural causes.'

'Kennedy Gerrard. A slimy pig. Dead. I don't know how. Shot, stabbed, garrotted, all three? they're not saying, but dead all right. No one will miss him, I'll tell you that. But cops, cops, cops, crawling everywhere. They've put a path of metal plates in the hallway. No one allowed in or out except residents. A guy in uniform at the door, checking us in and out. And cops crawling around in white paper suits like they've just landed from a space ship.'

Faz came over with mugs of coffee and tea. Jack thanked him.

'The tall woman detective...' She took a sip of coffee.

Jack knew she was talking about Hayley but kept it to himself. The way of the snoop.

'She knew I was in the flat illegally.' Heidi waved a hand to signify the chaos around her. 'She had the Council list. Soon as she told me who the actual tenant was, well, I couldn't say I was a guest, could I? That was a lie too easily cracked, by any of the other residents.'

A thought hit him.

'Who's your landlord?' he said.

She waved a hand. 'It's complicated.'

He tried again. 'Who do you pay your rent to?'

She took a sip of tea and hesitated. Jack caught a whiff of perfume. She was attractive, even more so when excited. He would like to run his fingers through her hair, and then maybe other places. He put his hands on his knees, to keep them there. Don't forget Xavier the octopus.

'Kennedy Gerrard,' she said at last.

'He's everywhere.' It had come to him as a possibility, the edge of remote.

'I pay my rent to Kennedy Gerrard,' she said. 'Well, I did. And a month's rent was due this week. So that's some savings, but a new place will need a deposit...'

He was processing her statement. Kennedy Gerrard was taking her rent.

'Who did he kick out?' he said.

'A Mr Greene. Mail comes sometimes. I pass it to Kennedy. He probably tears it up. Used to. Did. You know what I mean.'

'He has taken over two flats in the block?' It was hard to take in. 'Kennedy Gerrard took over two flats and no one has called the police.'

'Three flats,' she said. And laughed mirthlessly. 'Another one on the top floor. The Ballards left in a hurry around three months ago. Still empty.'

'Three!' exclaimed Jack. 'And none of the tenants have called the law?'

'Easy for you to say,' she scoffed. 'You've never met him. Luckily, you never will. A cold, calculating bastard. He smacked me round the face once when I said I needed a repair. "No repairs," he said. I got the message and paid for it myself.'

'But you stayed.'

She shrugged. 'The path of least resistance. I've got to live somewhere. All I had to do was pay him the rent once a month. Cash. He never tried it on with me, thank God. I'm too old for him, he's into young girls. But the irony is...' she gave a half laugh, 'now he's gone, I've got to go. He won't hit me any more, but the Council know I'm there illegally. That tall cop, she said, how did she put it?' Heidi thought for a second then added, '*The Council will be investigating all tenancies.* I've been shopped. Mr Greene will be back. God bless him, but I've got to find somewhere before they put me out on the street.'

'Hence the smart gear.'

'Respectable nurse wants a flat.' She sighed. 'Sorry to lay my troubles on you.'

She put a hand on his. Jack turned his over and held her fingers. She was looking into his eyes, he into hers. Was there trouble in the depths? Of course there was. But that had never stopped him. He was a port in a storm, so was she for that matter. They knew each other. Perhaps. For that instant they thought they did.

She said, 'You haven't got a spare room, have you?'

'I've a one bedroom flat,' he said. 'And my daughter stays over sometimes.'

She grimaced. 'But if I was really stuck?'

He thought rapidly. Her perfume, her body, the depth of her eyes. But bashing into each other in the kitchen and bathroom, the complication of Mia. It couldn't work. She was squeezing his fingers. He squeezed back.

'If you're really desperate,' he said, 'then OK.'

This was his chance, he should ask her...

'You were going to invite me over,' she said.

She was ahead of him.

'Yes.' His brain smothered in glue, words unable to get out.

'How about tonight?'

Chapter 17

Hayley was at the door of flat 4. Fayyad was in flat 3 opposite, interviewing the occupants. They'd agreed she should interview Mrs Nawaz, as being religious she wouldn't allow him in their home without her husband present. And as the husband was a taxi driver who seemed to work all hours, that would not be easy to arrange.

She took the phone from the pocket of her leather jacket and rang the number she'd been given by the housing office.

'Hello?' came a nervous query.

'Good afternoon. Are you Mrs Nawaz?'

'I am. Who are you?'

'I'm Detective Constable Hayley Amis. I'm outside your front door. We are interviewing everyone in the block about Kennedy Gerrard.'

'The man who was murdered?'

'Yes, Mrs Nawaz. You're not a suspect, but we need to learn as much as possible about him. So if I could come in and speak to you...'

'Have you got ID?'

'Yes.' Hayley fished out her warrant card.

'Hold it up to the spy hole please. A little closer. Yes, I see. Detective Constable Hayley Amis, Forest Gate police station. Stand back please, so I can see your face.' Hayley took a step back. 'You're not in uniform?'

'No, Mrs Nawaz. I'm a detective investigating the murder. And we don't wear uniform.'

'No man is with you?'

'I'm alone.'

'Wait a minute, I'll open the door.'

There were sounds of unlocking. Hayley looked down at her trainers, they were scuffed from the dust in the hall, she brushed one on the leg of her trousers, then the other. And then, irritated by the dust marks, knelt to brush the dust off the ankle with a tissue. She never wore skirts, or heels for that matter, being tall enough, and why be encumbered in a chase?

There were two locks, she noted. A bolt was shot at the top, and the sound of a chain being unhooked and falling. One lock being turned, then the other. The door opened. Before her stood a dark brown woman, a little below medium height, plumpish, with black hair resting on her shoulders. She was wearing light green shalwar kameez with a brown paisley pattern.

'Please come in.'

Mrs Nawaz held the door for her and Hayley stepped inside. She bent down to take off her shoes, knowing the drill for Asian households and having no wish to offend. She put them by the shoe rack along the wall which had assorted male and female shoes.

Mrs Nawaz smiled at Hayley's solicitude.

'Please come into the kitchen. I'll make you a cup of tea...' She hesitated. 'Shall I call you detective?'

'Yes, that's fine,' she said, knowing it better to keep things formal, rather than first names.

She followed Mrs Nawaz along the short hallway and into the kitchen. The room was light, with a pleasant aroma of spices. A window was open to the lawn of the back garden. To the side the fire escape could just be seen.

'Please sit down, detective. I'll put the kettle on.'

Hayley sat at the wooden table. There were four dark wood, high-backed chairs. She took out her notebook and placed it on the table with a pen as Mrs Nawaz filled the kettle.

She began with identification. She already had names and ages from the housing office, but she and Fayyad had quickly realised the authorities were ignorant of the sub-letting that went on. Mrs Nawaz put some biscuits on the table, giving them each a small plate. And then joined Hayley.

'How well did you know Kennedy Gerrard, Mrs Nawaz?'

She screwed her face. 'I kept well out of his way. He was a horrible man. There used to be that nice Asian young man in the flat, a Pakistani boy. He had some health troubles, had to use a wheelchair some days. Mr Gerrard forced him out and took over.'

'How do you know that?'

'Amir was his name. Always very polite. He just disappeared, and then Mr Gerrard was there. But one day, I was visiting my sister in East Ham and we went out shopping on High St North, and there I saw Amir. He told me what had happened. How Mr Gerrard smashed his computer and TV, and beat him up. He said he would kill him if he wasn't gone by the next day. Can you believe that? Here, in these flats. It's why I have all these locks.'

'We've spoken to Amir,' said Hayley. 'Once we are done here, Amir can have his flat back.'

'Will he want it? All those bad memories. Poor young man. Disabled too. You would think he had enough on his plate without having to deal with a monster like Mr Gerrard.'

Hayley couldn't disagree. Yesterday she had spoken to Amir at his parents' home in East Ham. And he wasn't keen on coming back. Gerrard had terrified him, and he was fearful of it happening again.

'I shouldn't say this,' said Mrs Nawaz, 'but I would con-
gratulate whoever killed him.'

'Violent men make enemies,' said Hayley carefully. 'Did
you know any of Mr Gerrard's visitors?'

Mrs Nawaz was pouring the tea and stopped.

'There was that layabout Sol. Fancy letting your son visit
that man. That's Mitzi from flat 3, opposite this one. A
Jamaican woman. I think she might be a prostitute, always
wearing these short skirts. Can you believe this place! No
wonder Amir doesn't want to come back. Though I haven't
seen Mitzi for a week or more. She lives with her son and
her brother. Funny name. Knocker. Can that be a proper
name?'

'Probably a nickname, I should think.'

'And I saw that Heidi from number 2 go into Mr
Gerrard's a few times.'

'Any idea why?'

'I don't know about English women, if you'll excuse me,
detective. They seem to go anywhere, do anything. Drugs,
maybe sex. What a world this is! I wouldn't go into his flat
myself, not for a thousand pounds. Bad enough to have to
walk by. It smells of wickedness. I always see my daughters
to the door of the block. I don't want them kidnapped. We
say hello. Well, you have to do that, but we don't mix with
the people here. We have our family, we have the mosque.
And to tell you the truth, I wish we were living somewhere
else.'

Hayley wasn't here to pass judgement. On a conservative
Muslim family or the lives of those who lived in the block,
providing they kept more or less within the law. She glanced
at her list of questions.

'What do you know about the fire, Mrs Nawaz?'

'Nothing until the fire brigade came. Our door was
locked, the curtains drawn. My eldest daughter thought she

could smell burning, but we thought it was just cooking, someone burnt a pan or something. But then someone was hammering on the door and yelling. We didn't know who it was and wondered whether to call the police. My husband was out with the taxi. But then I saw the yellow helmet through the spy hole. We all had to leave by the fire escape. And went to stay with my sister in East Ham for two days, till they let us back here. Do you think there's a connection, the fire and the murder?'

Chapter 18

'You're not on the tenancy agreement, Mr Baldwin,' said Fayyad. He was seated on a wooden chair facing a battered brown sofa that seated Sol and the man he was addressing. The room was untidy, clothing bundled here and there, a pile of fast food trays, their smell mingled with that of cannabis.

'I'm Knocker, no one calls me Mr Baldwin.'

He smiled through gapped teeth. His brown face was gaunt, almost skeletal, his hair shaved off his skull. He had a gold ring in one ear.

'The tenant is Mitzi Baldwin according to the Housing Department,' said Fayyad consulting his notebook. 'Where is she?'

'I'm her brother. She went off with a Nigerian fella. A week ago. She asked me to keep an eye on Sol here.'

The youth smiled when his name was mentioned.

'Shouldn't you be at school?' said Fayyad.

'I'm nineteen, mister,' he said affronted. 'I left school ages ago. Crap bin, Forest Gate. I've never been so bored in my life. They treat you like kids.'

He was tall like his uncle, wiry, his skin smoother, black hair twisted into dreadlocks. He was wearing a dirty t-shirt, with an aggressive head design, which Fayyad considered might be a rap star.

'You working?'

'I'm looking.'

Fayyad wondered how hard.

'And you, Knocker? How do you manage?'

'I got an injury.' He rubbed his back to demonstrate. 'I was a football player. Goal keeper, semi pro. I got a trial for Spurs, but I did my back in. Some days I'm OK. Some days I can't get out of bed.' He indicated his nephew. 'The boy's my carer. I couldn't manage without him.'

Questions were crossing Fayyad's mind, like who cared for you before you came here? And if the youngster got a job, what would you do then? But he was investigating a murder, not state benefit claims. Maybe Knocker did have a bad back. Maybe he'd had a trial for Spurs. There were just too many liars for him to take on anyone's claim without better evidence than their say so.

Fayyad's wife had said to him, you don't trust anyone any more.

True, true.

'Why Knocker – where'd that come from?' he said.

Knocker grinned, pleased at being the centre of attention.

'When I was a goalkeeper, I used to punch the ball a lot. Rather than catch it. *Knock it out here, knock it out there*, they'd shout at me. You must take care not to knock it to an attacker. Or bang, they score. Mind you, you don't always have the choice, ball coming at you high, you dive, just about get your fist to it, knock it wherever you can and hope.'

He laughed, reliving a save of twenty years ago.

'What's your actual first name?' said Fayyad.

'Matthew, but nobody calls me that now. Except Mitzi, but she's gone with that Nigerian.'

'Got a name for him?'

'No.'

'Have you, Sol?'

'No.'

'OK,' he said, sceptical about his unnamed Nigerian. The lack of any detail sowed doubt. He glanced down at his notebook. Down to the real business of the day. 'How well did you know Mr Kennedy?' he said. And caught a glance between the two of them. Did it mean an agreed story?

'Me first, Knocker?' asked Sol.

'You go,' said his uncle.

Sol sat up as if this was a job interview.

'Kennedy was a good guy. Always friendly. A handshake when he saw me. He always asked me about the family. From time to time, he'd invite me into his place. We'd smoke a bit of weed. Not a lot.' He indicated with forefinger and thumb just how minuscule. 'Play music. Play cards. I used to run errands for him.'

'What did you get for him?'

'Beer. I'd buy him a paper most days. He was a Sun reader.'

'Where did he get his weed from?'

'I never asked him.'

'What do you know about the fire, Sol?'

'Only there was one. I was in bed.'

'The boy was,' declared Knocker. 'He was in bed. I was in bed,' said Knocker. 'The fire brigade got us up and out. My back was killing me for two days after running down the fire escape.'

He began rubbing his back with both hands as if talk of the night of the fire had brought back the pain.

'Where did you stay for the couple of days you weren't allowed back?'

Knocker sucked his cheeks and rolled his shoulders. He said, 'Bed and breakfast. Romford Road.'

'Who paid?'

'I did. Like you said, I am not the legal tenant in this flat. So I had to pay for the two of us. A couple of hundred it cost me. So believe me, I want you to catch who started that fire and get two hundred quid off them for me.'

Sol was grinning to himself. What does he know, wondered Fayyad.

'Have you heard from your mother?' he asked the youngster.

'No.'

'Do you expect to?'

'Maybe.'

'You don't seem concerned.'

Sol shrugged. 'She gives me a lot of grief. Always nagging at me about a job, about staying out late. So maybe a break from her is all right.'

'Is that her picture?'

He indicated a photo in a frame on the cluttered mantelpiece. It showed the head and shoulders of a smiling black woman in her thirties, an age difficult to pinpoint, still youthful without signs of age. Her hair was an ornate style with small braids.

'That's her.'

'How old is she?'

'Thirty two,' said Knocker. 'Seven years younger than me. Baby sister.' He smiled. 'She's cute, yeh?'

'She must have been young when she had you.'

Sol shrugged. Not a fair question, Fayyad had said it too quickly. What could the youngster do about his mother's teenage pregnancy? He changed tack.

'You OK for money, Sol?'

'Gonna give me some?' He grinned at Fayyad, a mild challenge.

Fayyad reckoned Sol had cash from somewhere. He might be wearing a grubby t-shirt, but those Nike trainers weren't cheap. And bought recently.

'He's my carer,' said Knocker.

'Any other sources of income, Sol?'

'No.'

'You, Knocker. Just state benefits?'

'That's all I get. I survive. Look at this place. You think I got some secret stash?'

Fayyad couldn't help a grin. 'Doesn't look like it.'

Though he knew you couldn't tell. If you had cash coming in, you don't want to advertise. Then again, Sol's trainers. And his uncle had a slick pair too. Suggesting a family shopping trip, but with more than state benefits.

Fayyad glanced at his notes.

'A group of youngsters regularly used the foyer for smoking weed. Were you one of them, Sol?'

'Sometimes. But I didn't start the fire, if that's what you're asking. Why burn my own house down?'

'Do you know why Mr Kennedy should have been killed?'

The youth shook his head. 'He was a decent guy. Honest to goodness. Generous. He shared everything. Someone crazy must have killed him.'

Chapter 19

An OK afternoon. Jack was home. Heidi had come into the café and things had moved on. They'd got as far as holding hands, a small step. Not quite like stepping on the moon but it had points in common. She was coming to his place tonight, he'd been about to ask her, but she got in first.

Wahey!

Don't rush, he told himself. Be wary. You never know in these matters. Sex is one thing, a person and her problems are another. And they don't always gel. But the needy part of himself had run ahead, to holidays, to a house with roses round the front door, to loving arms greeting him after a hard day's work.

Love shmuv. Sentimental twaddle. He was too old to be taken in.

No, he wasn't.

He'd been smiling as he drove down to the dump at Jenkins Lane, and got rid of the rubbish from his lock-up. Still warm and cosy as he drove over to Manor Park to the locksmith and bought a hardened steel lock. It cost £45, which he handed over with reluctance. Quite a bite out of the money he had left.

He counted his cash on the kitchen table. Two tens, a fiver and some coins, amounting to £27.70. He searched his pockets and came up with a few extra coppers. So where was he? A date tonight. Yeh, yeh, apart from that. In work and OK for food. He didn't have a ladder but knew where he could borrow one, and had enough for tonight's takeaway, which was lots better than it had been earlier that day before the guttering work came in. The break-in at his lock-up came out of the blue, but the building game had taught him that there was always the unexpected about to drop on you.

Like Heidi coming into the café.

Didn't he owe Mia some money? Well, she'd have to wait. He wasn't due to see her until the weekend. Days and days away. He was maxed out on his overdraft and credit card, so tomorrow, he'd ask Ben for a sub. Things weren't that bad money-wise. Just tight for the time being, but money was due. There should be four weeks' work at Cromer Court. Maybe five or six if Tony continued to be as useless as he was yesterday.

Jack was just out of the shower when the phone rang. He'd been singing along to Garbage's *Run, Baby, Run* and contemplating Heidi's visit. Music off, he sat on the bath in nothing but a towel. Could this be work? If so, play the respectable builder, not the naked swain on the edge of the bath.

Not work. Alison.

'Hello, Alison. Can I do you a new roof?'

'I wouldn't mind a new daughter. Mia hasn't been in school today.'

'I drove her there.'

'She evidently didn't go in. The school phoned me. She was expected for her cello exam. The examiner was there. And she wasn't. I have no idea where she is. I've tried phoning her half a dozen times. And she won't answer my calls.'

Jack almost grinned at this. His daughter was obviously delaying her reprimand. Too serious for a grin.

'Did she practise last night?' went on Alison.

He could see how this was going. Alison was out to blame him.

'Yes, she did.' He defended himself, she wasn't going to load it on him. 'A good practice.' He wasn't going to tell her about the jazz session at Ben's. She'd think it inappropriate and find something to throw at him. He knew her of old.

'She's thirteen years old, wandering round with a cello, heaven knows where,' said Alison. 'She might pick up the phone if her indulgent father phoned her. Do you think?'

'I'll try, as soon as we finish this call.'

'Get back to me if you get in contact. Kids! Lord save me... I've two boys who've been fighting in class outside my door. Two minutes of mindfulness before I deal with the urchins. Bye.'

The call ended. Quite a blast, with Alison in arch head teacher mode. Fair enough in the circumstances. Where on earth was Mia?

He ruminated on the pluses and minuses of parenthood as he wiped himself. Mia had helped him out by going to Ben's last night. He enjoyed their trips out on the Flats with the telescope. But now she'd gone AWOL, dashing all her Brownie points.

She'd entered his mind too when Heidi had mentioned the possibility of staying at the flat a while. Children complicate your love life. Did Heidi mean it?

Forget daydreams with Heidi. He had an errant daughter to deal with.

He dressed. Why had she bunked off? Mia had practised last night, and did some first thing in the morning too. All signs she was going to take her cello exam. Something struck him; he hadn't thought to give her lunch money this morning, or get her a packed lunch. Surely she would have asked him if she hadn't any money. Or maybe she was as forgetful as he was.

Pathetic. Alison had a point.

All in the past, no point beating himself up about lunch money. The school would have paid for it if she'd had no money, and then phoned Alison. His fault. Always something. He combed his hair and rubbed his cheeks. He needed a shave before Heidi came, but he had to make the phone call. Either his daughter would answer or he'd be blocked too.

Still in the bathroom but clothed, Jack dialled. The phone to his ear, he waited the few seconds for the dial tone, wondering whether it would be responded to. And then heard ringing from the sitting room. God, she hadn't left her phone here? No, that didn't make sense.

Jack burst out of the bathroom.

And there was Mia, a little grubby in her school clothes. The cello was on the sofa beside her with her school bag.

'Where have you been?' he exclaimed.

'I bought you a cake,' she said, indicating the plate in the centre of the sitting room table, filled with a round coffee and walnut cake.

'You haven't been to school today,' he persisted.

'I have.'

He looked at the clock on the sideboard. She'd timed it properly. School had finished and this was about the time she'd get here, if coming straight here.

'The school phoned your mum,' he said. 'You haven't been in all day. So why, where, what for?' All the questions squeezed in his head flew off like freed doves.

Mia blew her cheeks out. Her long hair was straggly, in desperate need of a brush. He waited. She was working out whether to continue with the lie, looking up at the ceiling as if something might pop out and assist her.

She waved her hands furiously to keep the world off. He could see she was close to tears.

'You didn't want to take the cello exam,' he said. 'Did you?'

'You wouldn't listen. Neither you nor Mum. So I thought you would have to if I didn't take the exam.'

'We're listening now,' he said. 'Would it really have been so bad? I'm sure you could have taken the exam and passed without any trouble.'

She shrugged. 'I could have done. Sure. And then what? More scales, more arpeggios. More exams. On and on we go forever until I'm a soloist with the Berlin Philharmonic or begging on skid row.'

He quelled a grin; the contrast in outcomes was somewhat dramatic.

'So you bunked off?'

'Yes. You dropped me off. I waited until you'd gone and headed into Stratford.'

'Did you have any money?' He looked at the walnut cake. All that rich cream and nuts. Obviously a bribe. He wouldn't mind a cup of tea and cake. But serious parent interview first.

'You didn't give me any money, Dad. And I didn't have a packed lunch either. So I busked at Stratford Station.'

Jack was somewhat shocked, but he could hardly tell her off as he hadn't given her any money for lunch.

'Don't tell your mum you busked in Stratford. What did you play?'

'I played some jazz cello to begin with. And also the classical pieces I'd learnt for the exam.'

He almost approved. A classy busker.

'I had to sit on a wall,' she went on. 'It's almost impossible to play a cello standing up.'

'How much did you make?'

'A bit over eleven quid. Then security came and I had to go. I went to a café for lunch. Then to the Picture House. I sat in the front row, cello on the seat next to me. It was a mums and babies showing. Hard to concentrate on the film with all those babies bawling. They were changing nappies on the floor in front of me. Dead smelly with lotions and whatnot. But sort of suited the film.'

'What film was it?'

'Dunkirk.'

'Well, war is smelly.'

'And noisy, which it needed to be with all the racket in the audience. But all those bombs going off, big guns firing, the music swelling, a few babies crying almost fitted in.'

'Well, you've made your point,' he said. 'About the cello exam. But you are going to school tomorrow.'

'Yes, I am. Promise. Can I stay here tonight?'

A vision of him and Heidi shattered.

'You don't have any clean clothes,' he declared.

'I can put my pyjamas and dressing gown on and wash my clothes in the machine. Iron them too. Do some of yours while I'm at it.'

She could. Had done before. He couldn't argue there.

'I've got a date,' he said.

'Out, or is she coming here?'

'She's coming here.'

'You can't cook. Or nothing that would do for a date. I could make it.'

'We're having a takeaway.'

She thought for a second, a hand under her chin. 'I'll stay in the bedroom. I won't queer your pitch.'

He couldn't help a laugh at the too knowing expression. Then again, thirteen was getting there. But no way was she staying tonight.

'Let's have tea and cake,' he said amicably. 'Then I'll phone your mum.'

Chapter 20

Jack had gone into the kitchen to phone Alison, out of Mia's hearing. Alison's school had finished half an hour ago, and he caught her just before a staff meeting. She said she'd be over in an hour or so to pick up Mia.

Jack figured: fine, time enough for everyone to calm down.

If Mia stayed, that would put paid to his date with Heidi. She couldn't stay. How often did he have dates? He wasn't having a thirteen year old mess this up.

He'd have to side with Alison.

Mia was watching kids' TV; she dropped five years when she was upset. He made a pot of tea. And they had tea and cake in their separate territories. She on the sofa, he at the table flicking through his astronomy magazine. Though he was drawn to the TV programme, one of those ridiculous cartoons, where the wicked cat throws the mouse against the wall, hits it with a plank, and the mouse totters off seeing stars, and is right as rain ten seconds later, planning revenge.

A head made of rubber, bones unbreakable. No one dies, no one paralysed for life from the neck down. Wounds heal in seconds. Not that different from superheroes, he reflected. Batman might swing down from a skyscraper but he'd be so easy to annihilate if the Joker ceased joking and used a semi-automatic.

Tea over, he did some clearing up. His date was going to go ahead. It had to. He even got as far as changing the sheets; as it was quite likely the bedroom would be in use. Xavier the octopus, he couldn't help thinking of him.

Unwelcome arms. So difficult to know how fast you could go. Too fast and it's Xavier. Too slow and it's all chat and no action.

Better the latter on a first date. But Mia would have to go off with Alison. No ifs, no buts.

He hesitated with the vacuum cleaner, being handier with the electric drill. A quick whip round wouldn't do any harm. He plugged in and switched on. Useless. The bag was bunged up with dust. Did he have a new bag?

A few minutes' search told him that he didn't. He could of course empty the old one and re-use it. But there are limits and Jack had reached his. He put the vacuum cleaner back in the cupboard. He'd buy some new bags when he had some cash, when he remembered. And went over the carpet picking up visible dirt with his fingers.

Too much cleaning is bad for your health, he'd read in the Daily Mirror. It makes you less resistant to germs. Jack didn't believe everything he read in the papers but that article fitted his philosophy. So it must be true. Dirt is good for you. OK, Ben and Tony had gone too far, not that much grunge, but some makes you stronger.

It was recalling Ben and Tony's place that got him to have another go with the vacuum cleaner. The Wilsons' black and greasy kitchen floor, the dirty dishes piled to the taps in the sink, made him see his flat in someone else's eyes. And he removed the vacuum cleaner bag. It was, as anticipated, bulging with dust, causing him to sneeze. He rushed the bag outside and tipped its contents into the dustbin until it was flat and vapid.

He put the bag back on the vacuum cleaner just as Alison arrived. She was surprised at his antics, not surprised that he wasn't about to use it. The vacuum cleaner was ready for next time, he said.

Whenever that might be.

He made more tea. Alison turned the TV off. They were set for the family chat.

Alison had a strong face, did the job make it? Or had it been right for the job? She'd never been a pushover even in their early days. She was tough, maybe that came with knowing your mind. And now tanned from her half term holiday in Tenerife. Jack had to admit, she wasn't ageing badly. Her straight chestnut hair, unfussy, just touched her shoulders. Like her daughter she always wore trousers, and flat shoes, not deigning to wear what she called 'party shoes' for work. Though she had a pair in her office cupboard gathering dust.

Mia was on the sofa awaiting the deluge, Jack and Alison brought over chairs from the table so they could be facing each other. Jack poured out the tea and handed the cups round as Alison posed the big question.

'So where have you been all day, Mia?'

Alison knew some of the answer, as Jack had told her briefly over the phone, but Mia filled in the detail. And when pushed by her mother, admitted busking, as only the truth would convincingly fill the hours of the day.

'All to skip a cello exam?' said Alison with a sigh.

'Yes,' said Mia, avoiding her mother's eye.

'It's not a good strategy, skipping exams.' The head teacher talking, thought Jack. 'If you get into the habit, you'll leave school without qualifications. And then where will you be? Look at your father.'

That hurt. True, he'd left school taking few exams. But need she rub it in, in front of their daughter?

'He fixed our plumbing,' said Mia. 'Which just goes to show you don't need exams for everything.'

He ought to take an exam in something, he thought. Astronomy or mathematics, just to show her. An evening class somewhere. He really should, instead of thinking about it.

'And I don't want to be a professional cellist,' added Mia.

'Or be an historian, or a mathematician,' added her mother, 'or a Spanish interpreter, or a writer, or a scientist...'

'I might want to be a scientist.'

'They take exams, you know. They don't bunk off.'

'You don't need cello exams to be a physicist.'

'Einstein played the violin.' Alison looked to Jack. 'Am I right?'

'You are.'

He was pretty sure she was. That sounded like an Einstein thing, violin playing. Best to back Alison up. In spite of her low blow.

'Playing the fiddle had nothing to do with his science,' said Mia.

'How do you know?'

'He didn't get the Nobel Prize for violin playing.'

'But who's to say, it didn't contribute?'

'You don't know, I don't know. Einstein has nothing to do with today.'

Jack was trying not to smirk. Einstein was definitely off-piste. Even head teachers can't always stick to the point.

'We can't make you take cello exams,' said Alison, giving up on the Nobel laureate. 'But it will mean you'll have to give back the cello.'

'Why?'

'Because they expect you to take music exams.'

'Stéphane Grappelli didn't take exams.'

Smart, thought Jack. He knew Alison had some of his recordings.

'I bet he did,' said Alison.

'No, he did not,' said Mia firmly. 'He was self taught. He played jazz at the Hot Club de France. He didn't play any classical music. Though he did play with Yehudi Menuhin. But that was just a jazz improvisation. And Menuhin said Grappelli was a better improviser than he was.'

'It's school rules,' insisted Alison, letting the Menuhin point pass, as it just might be true. 'You have to take the exams to have music lessons,' she added.

'I don't need lessons,' said Mia. 'I'll be self taught.'

'It's a school cello!' exclaimed Alison. 'They make the rules, they'll take it off you.'

'Not if you tell them.'

'What should I tell them?'

'That I am going to keep playing the cello, but without lessons.'

Alison shook her head. 'I can't see them agreeing to that. One rebel and then everyone gives up lessons. Fine example. And please, don't argue with me. I'm a head teacher. I know how it goes.'

Jack looked at the women in his life. Both had set out their stalls. How alike they were in temperament and appearance. Same chestnut hair colouring, though Alison's hair was tidy, her daughter's straggly and needing a brush. Mia was almost the same height as her mother, her figure filling out. The same stubbornness.

'I'll play you some jazz,' said Mia, not to be beaten. 'Do you want to hear me?'

'This is not the time...' began Alison.

'Play some,' said Jack, touching Alison lightly on the arm. Though wondering even as the words came out. Last night had been rather a caterwaul. 'We'll have more tea and cake.'

'You shouldn't encourage her.'

'It's not as if she doesn't want to keep playing.'

'They'll take away the cello.'

'One thing at a time. Let's have tea and a listen.'

While her parents talked over her, Mia had taken out the cello from its case. Jack went into the kitchen to put the kettle on, and Mia took his chair and set herself up, with the cello between her knees. She played a couple of notes with the bow and winced. Mia tightened and loosened the wooden screws. She played the notes again, then satisfied, she set off, playing *When the Saints Go Marching In*.

Jack returned and sat on the sofa.

She was notably better than last night. There was no poor piano player to hold her back, and she'd had a lot of practice today busking at Stratford. The music had a playful lightness, busy, fast. She was on her own, having had two hours' practice at the station. A practised improvisation, almost a contradiction, but with confidence to know where you might head off to. Jack waited for jangles and hesitation. But there weren't any. She returned to the melody and began singing. Alison hesitated and then, seduced, joined in with her warm contralto. Jack couldn't sing, but what the hell.

Who was going to notice?

A family sing-song, the cello an odd instrument for it, but Mia had put in the practice, even if illicitly.

Mia stopped for a second, halting the singers, and improvised round the tune, away, almost back to it, away once more, and suddenly without stopping she segued into *Drunken Sailor*. Better than last night.

Which had taught her how not to do it. Several hours busking had paid off. Though he wasn't going to say so. Bunking off, he agreed with Alison, is not to be encouraged.

Mia stopped playing, and looked at her parents, especially her mother, wondering if her savage breast was soothed.

'I'll talk to your head,' said Alison.

Chapter 21

Mia left with Alison, to Jack's relief. Jack accompanied them to the front door and went back upstairs. And felt abandoned. Hadn't he wanted Mia to go with Alison? Yes. And no. He couldn't win. He wanted family, he wanted his date. Incompatibles.

Split families. That was the way it was. Mia was here when he didn't want her to be, and not when he wanted her to be.

Rubbish, he told himself. Hadn't things worked out the way he had wanted them to? He wanted Mia to stay with Alison.

And yet felt defeated.

He strolled about the sitting room in exasperation. No, he would not do any more cleaning. It was so temporary. In desperation, he picked up a book from the sideboard, one he'd taken out of the library, *Dust to Dust*, that he hadn't got round to reading. The title reminded him of his vacuum cleaner bag, but glancing at the chapter headings and photos, he could see it was about the life and death of stars. He read the first page of the introduction, heavy stuff. Stars formed from the dust in space, shone for billions of years and then exploded to dust. Dust everywhere. Carpets and hallways and deep space. Wasn't that what he was thinking about earlier? Things breaking down, dust, mess. Could that be applied to families? Argument, stress, loneliness even. Our lives, never going in a straight line, creating dust that we sweep away in our vain efforts to defeat the never ending breakdown of the universe.

He had a sudden thought on why the violin had helped Einstein. And he googled 'Einstein and the violin' on his laptop. And discovered that Einstein's mother pushed him to practise, which caused Jack to grin. As a child, Einstein found practising a chore until he discovered Mozart's violin sonatas when he was thirteen. Then he was hooked. Several sites said the same thing about his creativity: the balance of music and physics gave him his big ideas.

Though none said whether he took music exams. Einstein practised, he took lessons, but the answer to the big question, the Alison silencer: music exams, Jack could find no mention either way. Jack found a school report. It was small and in German. Did it say music studies or something like that? Even if it did, that didn't mean he took violin exams.

He stopped and wondered where he was going. How did music exams save you from the breakdown of the universe? They didn't, of course. It was music that did. It stopped you thinking about something that was beyond your power to do anything about. Making music involved fingers, voice and mind totally in creating harmony.

Was it too late for him to learn an instrument? But heaven forbid, he'd end up like Ben, an elephant at the keyboard. Therapy for Ben maybe, but an earache for the listener.

The doorbell rang. And Jack gave up his Einstein studies.

He went down the stairs, knowing who it must be. Heavens, he hadn't thought about food. The takeaway. He was so easily distracted. Well, he shouldn't order the takeaway himself anyway. He had no idea what she liked.

Plenty of dust on the stairs. Always there, waiting to ambush him. He could have swept the stairs, he'd had time and a working vacuum cleaner. Tomorrow.

There'd be more dust then. So all the better.

Heidi was at the door, in a red skirt and matching jacket and beret. Her perfume overwhelmed him. That's what being alone does for you. The signals, the signs, instant response.

He invited her up, again aware of the dust on the stairs. Too late. It wasn't until they were in the flat, casting off redness and perfume, that he thought again about the takeaway.

'I've had a busy afternoon,' he said. 'I didn't get a menu from Moon House. Maybe we should take a stroll down.'

'I've got one,' she said. And took it out of her red handbag.

They sat at the table. For some reason, Jack felt shy. She'd obviously taken care, her freckles were barely visible through her make-up, her lips a very orange red. It was her presence here, solid and sexual, when he barely knew her.

He could barely speak, as if his tongue had thickened. Mind clouded, he grasped a thought; they had no drink, beyond tea and tap water. They needed, more than life itself: fruit juice, fizzy water or some non-alcoholic concoction. Mia turning up, then Alison, and Einstein and the dusty universe had thrown it out of his head.

Redness and perfume pulsating, he managed to say, 'Let's go out, make the order at Moon House and pick up something to drink from the Co-op.'

'Non-alcoholic.'

He smiled, pleased she'd remembered, grateful he had some vocabulary.

They left the house. It was still light, and would be for another two hours, a midsummer evening, the sun in a glowing tumble of clouds to the west. She took his arm, and they strolled between the full trees on Earlham Grove. He felt the pressure of her arm on his. A welcome presence.

Walking eased his turbulence. His legs were hollow; taking one step at a time.

She said, 'What have you been doing this afternoon?'

'I had a shower.'

'I can see that,' she said. 'But you need a shave.'

She rubbed his chin, he felt it rasp against her fingers.

'I was about to shave when my ex phoned.'

He told her about Mia's escapade and her mother coming over. The words burbling like a mountain stream over stones. He could barely stop, rushing downhill, telling of mother and daughter going hell for leather. Of Stéphane Grappelli and Einstein and whether either of them took music exams.

'I took a back seat on that,' he said, managing to dam the babble.

'Oh, I used to argue with my mother, all the time,' exclaimed Heidi. 'It's inevitable. You're growing up, more your mother's size, hormones coursing. It'd be surprising if you didn't fight.'

'So how was your afternoon?' said Jack. 'You left me to go flat hunting.' Turning it over to her, as he was too edgy to be coherent.

'I went to three estate agents,' she said. 'I could have seen some flats tonight, but I didn't want to cancel being with you.' She squeezed his hand, he gripped back, half understanding her message.

The sun had come out of the clouds and their shadows stretched down the pavement. Long legs, short arms with tiny hands, and heads like blobs on a post.

'I know they'll be horrid,' she went on. 'It's a landlord's market. They can rent any old rubbish. At least at Cromer Court I have my own kitchen, sitting room and bedroom. All I had to do was keep out of Kennedy's way, just pay him my rent each month, which I did, promptly. Though he said it was going up a hundred a month from next month. I knew better than to argue. Not with Kennedy. It was either pay him or get out. As it was, I had to find another tenant to share the rent. But sooner or later, he would have squeezed me out.' She half laughed. 'A hundred more every month, and he would put it up again I'm sure. It couldn't go on. Just a question of when I'd go.'

She gripped his hand hard. 'Oh, you are stuck as a tenant. Landlords can get away with so much. It's such an effort to move, and they know it. Well, I have to move now. The Council will be on my case any day. They'll evict me if I'm still there. So I must pound the pavements, see all the places I don't want, knowing I have to take the least worst. What a pointless sweat.'

'Do you want me to come with you?'

'Not a good idea,' she said. 'Thank you for asking, but landlords will think we are a couple. And I want to be the respectable single lady. A nurse. Quiet, pays the rent on time, few visitors. Oh, I hate being judged like that.'

They had reached the high street and turned towards the Co-op.

Jack said, 'I could help you move. We could hire a small lorry for the day. Have to be at a weekend to fit in with work.' And Alison would have to have Mia. Hurried calculations, based on redness and perfume and being with Heidi.

'Thank you,' she said. 'When I've accepted a place, I'd be grateful for your help. But I don't want to talk about moving any more. I'll bore you stiff. And it's so pointless. I have to do it. That's all there is to it. Let's think about juice. Non-alcoholic stuff. I quite approve. I worked in casualty for three years, and we had to deal with drunks and the victims of drunks every night when the pubs shut. Stupid drunks who could hardly remember their own names. Or where they lived or where they'd put their fists.' She stopped. 'I'm talking too much. Do you know why?'

'Because you've got to move.'

'True, true, true, but it's also the company. I like being with you. Weird, as I hardly know you; I don't know what you're thinking.'

'Same old stuff, male thoughts men think. Disgusting heads we've got.'

She picked up a basket and they entered the Co-op.

'That's sex all over,' she said as they walked between the fruit and vegetables. 'It's natural. Hormones buzzing about, social conditioning, evolution. It's why we are going out together. Talking about everything else but.'

They had ground to a halt, bananas and oranges on one side, green leafy things on the other. A woman in a hijab was examining the sell-by date on watercress. Away ran the aisle, overhead fluorescent lighting showing the way.

'Your heart is not in this,' he said.

'Does it show?'

'It's obvious shopping is not to your liking.'

'I was doing it to be agreeable.'

'You have to shop some time.'

'Yes.' She looked desperately about her. 'Supermarkets are all the same. Aisles and aisles of food and people. A necessary invention, I'm sure. Fine for married couples for the weekly shop. But not for a date.'

'We could go to bed,' he said.

'Let's do that,' she said. 'A much better offer than fruit juice.'

Chapter 22

Jack rolled over. He was on the window side of the bed. The curtains had been drawn, he flipped up the end an inch.

'It's still light,' he said.

'Open them fully,' she said.

'Neighbours might complain.'

'I will then,' and she began to clamber over him.

He held her arms, she resisted for a few seconds, then slipped into an embrace, less urgent than their lovemaking. She broke away and endeavoured to fully open the curtains.

'There's no one in the garden to see us,' she said, the curtains half wide. 'And at the end, beyond the wall, there's another garden. They'd need binoculars.' She crawled over his thighs and groin opening the curtain on that side and then over his face, her hair and breasts gliding over him, to open the other curtain. 'I love the light, these long days.' She turned to him. 'You know what I really like?'

He waited, half suspecting bondage or an order for them to run round the garden naked like a latter day Adam and Eve.

'Tell me.'

She lay back on the pillow and took his hand, placing it on her stomach.

'Walks in the country.'

'Naked?'

'Of course not. I'd wear my boots.'

'Puss in Boots,' he said, smiling contentedly at the vision.

'He was a big cat, Puss was,' she hissed, showing her claws, and threatening to gouge his face. Instead, she sprung out of bed. 'I'm hungry. Have you got any mice in the fridge?' She picked up her clothes from the floor, clutching them to her chest. 'I shall pop out and have a look.'

He stretched for her as she left him for the sitting room.

Jack lay back, half satisfied. He would've liked to have chatted more, might be up to another round of sex in half an hour. But there were two involved, two compromises. Always the way.

Anyway, he was getting hungry. Another basic need.

Lazily, he sat upright and started to dress, putting on vest and pants and socks. And heard the roar of the vacuum cleaner. She wasn't, surely?

He flung open the bedroom door. Heidi was vacuuming, stubbornly naked, her clothes in a pile on the sofa. Like a soft porn film with him playing the window cleaner.

'Sex makes me active,' she exclaimed, thrusting the tube end under the sofa. 'And your carpet is badly in need of a clean. I was going to mention it earlier when we were rolling about, but it seemed rude.'

'Let me do it,' he said. 'I meant to.'

'No,' she said. 'I won't do this ever again. But please, don't stop me now.'

He felt helpless watching her activity. He should do something.

'I'll phone for the food.'

'I've done it,' she said. 'Meal for two, £14.50. Why don't you have a shave? You were rubbing me raw.'

'Nothing but complaints,' he said, heading for the bathroom.

While he shaved, he considered whether she was too dominant. The vacuuming, ordering the food, demanding he shave. Small things, but signs of things to come. He dismissed the thought, his habit of damning a relationship when it had hardly begun.

The food came and they ate. Heidi told him she was a member of a walking club. She went walking most weekends in the countryside, hospital shifts permitting.

'Can you map read?'

'I sure can, buddy. And take a mean compass bearing.' They had almost finished eating, the plastic trays scoured, and were drinking tea. 'You have a telescope, there.' She pointed. 'In the corner. Not the easiest thing to vacuum around.'

'I wasn't expecting anyone so eager.'

'When do I get to use it?'

'I'll go for a walk with you, and you come out on the Flats with my scope.'

'Agreed.' She stood up. 'And now I really must go.'

'Already? It's only nine thirty.'

'I'm on at six in the morning. I have to be up at five.'

'You could leave from here.'

'I wouldn't get much sleep, would I?' She didn't wait for his protestation. 'Besides, I can't go in wearing these clothes. Too tarty.'

She put her jacket on. He was thwarted, expecting a longer evening, with them spending the night together. But he could see her reasoning. Working life intervenes.

'I'll walk you home.'

Chapter 23

The sun had only just set when they left the house, the shadows gone in that interval of light with the sun barely below the horizon, the street lights not yet on, the day resisting bedtime like a recalcitrant child.

They walked arm in arm, crossing the road to the footbridge over the railway. The paved area before the bridge was in possession of a sofa, springs coming through the seating and back. The bridge ahead humped over the eight lines of railway track. On either side of its ascent, caged off areas were filled with takeaway garbage receptacles and household refuse. Jack wondered if anyone slept there as it offered some shelter under the rising bridge, from the weather and marauders.

'I'd never come over this bridge on my own at night,' said Heidi.

The footbridge was narrow, just two pedestrians wide. The section over the railway had riveted metal walls, which had been brightened with colourful paintings by school children some fifteen years ago, but was now very scratched.

'On my own, I imagine being in the middle,' she went on, 'with someone ahead and someone behind. You'd be trapped between them.'

'Do you go the long way round?'

'I do. Better than risking rape or getting mugged.'

She shivered against him.

'I don't think about it,' said Jack. 'My ex says I lack imagination.'

'A man was murdered in my flats,' said Heidi with a shiver. 'Unlikely things happen. When I was a teacher we had to risk assess any trip we took the children on. I'd risk assess this bridge at night. Avoid, avoid, avoid. Go the long way round.'

They were in the middle, the muralled sides cutting off any view of the track. A train rumbled beneath them, shaking the bridge. He let it rush through, before speaking.

'Any idea who killed him?'

They were at the end of the bridge, high enough to see the fiery clouds on the horizon, reminding him of her jacket when she was at the door blasting him with his own feelings.

Red is a sexy colour.

'That's exactly what the tall cop asked me. *Any idea who killed him?* Those very same words. You're in the wrong job, Jack.' She squeezed his hand. 'What could I say to her? This person, that person, going through the possibilities in the block.'

'What did you say?'

'I told her I had no idea. I said he had visitors, quite a few. Some of them underage girls. Short skirts and make-up with Uncle Kennedy offering sweets.'

They'd come down to Forest Lane, a busy road running along the railway line, one side with housing, a park and shops further up, and the other with a high brick wall to keep the reckless off the railway.

'It could be someone living in the flats,' he said.

She stopped and poked him in the chest.

'Are you trying to give me nightmares?'

'You could stay at my place.'

'I told you why not,' she said sharply.

They walked on, turning down a side road. A street lamp blinked on. She had not taken his arm again. Jack registered the rejection. He had been unsubtle.

'Sorry,' he said. 'Stupid of me. It's not as if I live there.'

'You don't,' she reminded him, and took his arm again. 'And I do. And of course it could be one of the residents. There's all sorts of things going on.' She gave a short laugh. 'One benefit of me moving, I'll be getting away from drug dealers and underage prostitutes.'

'That bad?'

'That bad.'

He thought again that she should stay at his place, but didn't say so. She was going home, she'd made up her mind.

She said, 'I enjoyed this evening. Thank you. And I don't want to spoil it by being a grouch. You took me out of myself.' She swung about and kissed him.

They embraced under a street light, arms round each other, fleeting heat in the universe's cold night. As they kissed, he attempted ESP through his lips. *Come back to my place.*

She broke away.

'I must get to bed. Need the sleep. I've a long shift tomorrow.'

They walked on and came to the block. Down the short path, a uniformed policeman stood at the door to the block. The hallway was fully lit.

'You've got temporary lighting,' said Jack.

'They put it in yesterday.'

He held her arm, to stop her running off. He must see her again.

'What are you doing tomorrow night?'

'Going out with you and your telescope.'

She pecked him on the cheek, twirled about, and strode down the path. Gone before he could say another goodbye, or what time, where. She was with the policeman; he was saying something that Jack couldn't hear. He continued watching as she pushed open the door, giving him a wave.

She'd turned away; the final goodbye. He was looking; she was not. There was a line of metal plates in the hall as if she were crossing a marsh, going from the front to the garden door. Heidi was at her door turning the key. She didn't look his way, but pushed the door and went inside.

Gone.

Just a single lock, he thought. But then she'd had Kennedy to protect her. Maybe she had bolts on the inside. Jack waved to the policeman who was watching him. And then reflected and went down the path to talk to him.

'Sorry, sir, but you can't go in. Just residents.'

He was a young man, broad and tall, in a peaked hat and uniform, smelling of aftershave.

Jack said, 'I don't want to go in. Just thought I'd have a word. I'm a builder here, pushed out by you lot.'

'Can't be helped,' said the policeman. 'Murder has to be investigated. You that friend of Fayyad's?'

'I am,' he said. 'He been talking about me?'

'I heard him say to his boss that he had eyes and ears on the inside. Have you solved it for us yet?'

'I'm only offering to help,' said Jack, uncomfortable. 'The odd word, any gossip. That's all.'

'You were out with the woman from number 2.'

'Nice lady. She didn't do it.'

The young cop waved a finger. 'Rule nothing out. That's what they say. Believe no one.' He laughed. 'But we're not robots yet.'

'Gotta go,' said Jack. 'You here all night?'

'Off in an hour, thank God.'

'See you.'

Jack turned away. And walked down the path to the street. The street lights had come on in the twilight.

Going home alone, but he couldn't complain. It had been a pleasant evening, which he would have liked to have gone on longer, but work intervenes, as it often does.

But she was coming out with him on the Flats tomorrow night.

He didn't know her. They'd made love, they'd talked. She'd been a teacher before she'd become a nurse. Had she anyone else in her life? Not impossible. She hadn't asked him, he hadn't asked her. An impertinence so early in their relationship. Such things can be kept back, separate compartments. Tell A nothing about B. Tell B nothing about A. He was no angel; it was why he distrusted others.

Was that a vice?

Possibly. But sex was sex, greedy, pushing others out of the way, like birds in a nest going for the worm. Trust takes time. It can be built, it can be broken.

But a good evening. OK, she had to leave early but he was content. There was a cop there making sure she had no other lovers. He laughed at his jealousy. She'd shared some things, he'd shared some. He recalled her vacuuming naked.

An elderly black man looked at him oddly, making him aware of his broad grin.

'Good evening,' he said, and passed the smile on. And got one back.

He had come to the railway bridge. The one Heidi hated. He walked up the slope, to where the bridge began its span over the road and the railway lines. At the high point, just before the crossing, he looked down the road. Cars were coming towards him, yellow headlights, those heading away with red tail lights. All the busyness of the world. Lights were on in the silhouetted tower block farther off. A half empty train clattered by, heading towards Maryland and Stratford. A pale blue light streaked the horizon, the last glimmer of the dying sun.

He turned and headed across the bridge, glancing at the scratched murals on the metal walls, so unnecessary. Why destroy?

Jealous of those who create. So maybe he should learn a musical instrument, be like Einstein and Mia. Guitar, keyboard, which?

He was struck on the head from behind. Jack turned to face his assailant, catching sight of a hooded shadow and an arm coming down holding something long and thick. He raised an arm to fend it off. Too late. He was struck again, and blacked out.

Chapter 24

'He's coming round.'

Jack opened his eyes. Who was coming round? Above him, bending down were a man with a grey beard and a stocky Asian woman in a green uniform.

'Where am I?' he said, knowing even as the words came out, it was a cliché. He was the assaulted gumshoe, the one coming round, the ground hard under his buttocks, metal at his back.

'You're on the railway bridge between Earlham Grove and Forest Lane,' said the woman. 'This man found you.' She indicated the man. 'And called us, the ambulance service. Have you been drinking?'

'No.' His head hurt at the back and front. He rubbed the mound at the back. It felt as big as a Brussels sprout.

'Do you know what happened?' said the paramedic.

'No, I don't.' He tried to think back from leaving Heidi at her block, talking to the cop, walking back, thinking about going on the Flats with her tomorrow. On the bridge looking at the lights of cars and buildings, the scratched panels, music and creativity. 'Someone hit me,' he exclaimed.

'You've been unconscious. We don't know how long for.'

'What's the time?'

'Six minutes to ten.'

'I left my house about 9.40, walked my girlfriend back to her place, not far. And came back.'

'Unconscious for just a few minutes then,' said the paramedic. 'I want to get you to the ambulance. And then get you to casualty. You're not a stretcher case. I'm going to fetch a wheelchair.' She said to the man, 'Will you stay with him? I'll only be a minute.'

'Sure.'

The paramedic left, walking rapidly.

'Thanks,' said Jack to the man. 'Do I know you?'

'I live opposite you. You're Jack of All Trades. I've seen your van running about.'

Jack smiled and then grimaced as pain shot through his skull. He managed to say, 'Thanks for stopping. Not everyone would.'

'I thought you were drunk, but I couldn't smell anything.'

'Thanks,' he said again, aware he was repeating himself. 'I wonder if I can get up.'

'No. Stay there,' said the man, a hand on Jack's shoulder. 'The paramedic is bringing a wheelchair. She knows what she's doing.'

'Yeh.' Jack stayed put, rubbing his throbbing skull. No rush. What had happened had happened. Leave it to the professionals.

On the walkway, there was a rumble and footsteps. The paramedic came into view pushing a wheelchair.

'Let's get you into this,' she said when she'd got to him. She knelt down, and put her hands under Jack's arms. 'Now easy does it. I'm going to pull you upright against the wall. Up we come, push with your legs.'

Jack pushed as the medic lifted under his arms.

'Easy does it. That's the way.'

Jack was upright, the world not quite steady, tipping back and forth.

'In the chair. Just relax. Good fellow.'

She settled him in the wheelchair, putting his feet on the step.

'If I can leave you now?' said the man, glancing at his watch. 'I'm rather late.' He tapped Jack on the shoulder. 'You'll be all right, Jack of All Trades.'

'Thank you,' said Jack.

And the man left them, heading off across the bridge.

'Let's get you to the ambulance,' said the paramedic, and began pushing him down the slope of the bridge.

Chapter 25

Jack was four hours at Newham General Hospital. Much of it spent waiting: for his examination, for an X-ray, for a doctor's verdict. His head throbbed throughout; there'd been bleeding which had scabbed over. The wound was cleaned and dressed by a nurse. During a waiting period, he searched his pockets. He still had his wallet which was a relief; he couldn't see anything taken from it. The money was still there, a maxed out credit card, no use to him or a thief. He had his phone too. It was on the old fashioned side, but good enough for him. Maybe not saleable.

But his keys were missing. He searched his pockets several times. They were on a fob with a compass: keys for the flat and keys for his van. Spares to the van were upstairs in the flat, spare keys to his flat were behind a loose brick in the bin area. His cunning plan, never yet put into action. At Alcohol Halt, there'd been a discussion about lost keys. Everyone in the circle had had the problem, coming home from a drunken spree with keys abandoned somewhere along the way, in a bar, on the street, in a taxi, down the drain. One time, Jack had had to smash in his flat door, resulting in a complete replacement of door and surrounds. Mia had a set these days but prior to that he'd taken precautions.

All the clever plans discussed at Alcohol Halt, under flowerpots, not so clever, in sheds, buried, so long as you remembered where. Jack had chiselled an inch off the back of a brick from the bin area. In the recess he'd put his house keys: the one for the house door and the other to his flat.

And put the brick back. That was eighteen months ago; he'd never had to use them.

He hoped he could find the brick and get it out. Or was it in a dream that he'd even put his keys there? Had he taken them out since? Jack wasn't thinking clearly, limited in brain capacity by the blows on the head.

He hoped the keys were still there, but couldn't be sure. Might they be the set he gave to Mia? So hard to think.

At the hospital, he'd been offered a cup of tea and was able to drink it slowly and nibble a couple of biscuits. His head was throbbing, there were swellings at the top of his head and at the back. A nurse had given him pain killers which worked to an extent.

A young doctor came at last, in a white coat holding the X-ray plate. He told Jack he couldn't see any serious damage. He asked a few questions. And Jack confirmed that he had no double vision or vomiting. When asked, he scored one hundred percent for the name of the reigning monarch, the Prime Minister and the date. He was told to go home, take things easy for a day or two. And phone 999 if he began having memory problems, dizziness or vomiting.

Jack thanked the doctor and went to reception. There, he enquired about a lift home, and was told it could be a couple of hours. Jack was unwilling to wait as it was already past 3 am. Reception pointed out a public phone which was connected to a local taxi firm.

Unwilling to fork out half his cash, Jack set off walking.

Outside the hospital, there was a sheltered smokers' area where a couple of dressing gowned patients, even at this hour, puffed their smoke of choice. The night was chilly, the more so having come out of a warm hospital. He zipped his jacket to the neck, sunk his hands into his pockets and began striding out, but quickly found his throbbing head wouldn't allow the speed. He slowed to an easier pace.

He walked down Prince Regents Lane to the Barking Road. There was little traffic, a breeze, the main roads brightly lit. He crossed over and walked up Greengate Street, every so often stopping to rest on a low wall, breathing deeply and massaging the dome of his head. The doctor had told him to take a couple of days off work. That wasn't his plan, not with his finances. He must be at work tomorrow. Not tomorrow, he corrected himself, this morning, in four and a half hours to be exact.

How he would cope was another matter. But get home first, and find the door keys.

Walking past the high railings of West Ham Park, he was aware of seeing double. A bright image of the lamp post ahead and a lighter one parallel to it. Temporary, he hoped. His headache was a little worse, but he had painkillers at home. Not far to go. By trial and error, he'd developed a technique of walking, keeping as upright as possible like a puppet, that minimised the throbbing.

He was shivery, possibly had a temperature; a two mile walk wasn't what the doctor ordered. Should he have a cup of tea, or slump straight into bed to make the best of the few hours left?

Decisions, decisions, foot one before foot two. Then vice versa. Repeat.

At last, he got to the house. He came into the path, and pulled out one of the bins. And by the light of his phone, on his knees, explored the brickwork. He found the one, probably the one, and couldn't get the brick out. It should be the one, there was little mortar round it. But after eighteen months of weathering, it had set in hard. He needed a lever. He rose too quickly, setting his head off. Taking deep breaths, he relaxed against a bin for half a minute before searching for a piece of wood, some bit of metal, he could use to lever the brick out.

Under the porch of his house, he found his keys.

That should have concerned him, but he was too tired to worry, to care at all, grateful for the keys in his hand. Jack opened the house door and then his flat door. He went up the stairs. Had he left the light on? He must've done. And opened the sitting room door.

It was in full light, and turned upside down. Every drawer was emptied, the cupboard pulled out, the cushions off the sofa and on the floor. Plainly he'd been burgled. He looked to his telescope in a corner, one of his few valuables, and crossed to it. The instrument was on its side but seemed to be OK. His laptop was on the floor. He put it on the table.

Clearly this wasn't a regular burglary. The intruder had been looking for something in particular. The kitchen was a tip, drawers turned over, cupboards wide open, as was the bedroom. Jack lacked the energy to begin the clear up. It was past 4 am. He straightened the bed, set the alarm for 7.30, switched off the light, and the sight of the mess.

And got into bed.

Chapter 26

The alarm went off. Jack lay in the warmth, half awake, his body stiff, the two mounds on his head too present. Three times he pressed the snooze button. At the fourth ring, he reluctantly got up.

The mess around struck him. He'd forgotten about the burglary. But this wasn't the time for tidying. He took off his shirt and trousers and put them on the chair by the bed. He'd got into bed without undressing but not in working clothes, wearing those he'd worn for Heidi's visit. Half amused at undressing when just out of bed, he picked up a pair of paint splattered work jeans and a rumpled t-shirt.

Once dressed, he put the kettle on, and had a cursory wash. Cleaning his teeth wobbled his head too much, and so he gave up on it. A quick coffee, which he took into the sitting room amid the debris. A sock drawer that had been emptied onto the floor. Half the socks should go, they had holes in the heels. He could pair up the odd ones, some day, some time.

It was a measure of his tiredness that the mess seemed normal. He put his boots on and left the house.

Driving to the site, he had a trace of double vision. His head was aching but it was difficult to abstract it from drowsiness as he'd spent much of the time in bed awake rather than sleeping.

What excuse would he make to Ben at his lateness? It was like school; he should forge a note from his mother.

Tell him the truth? That he'd been hit on the head and had to go to hospital. And didn't get home till gone four in the morning. But Ben might send him home. No, Ben wouldn't, he was desperate to get the job moving, but he would be watching him for signs of weakness.

And then might send him home, if his work rate was pathetic.

He didn't want to be watched, hoping somehow he'd get away with it. Though he didn't know how he'd function. He could say that the van wouldn't start, and he had to clean the plugs, that was as good as anything. He'd get a reprimand, he'd apologise, the usual, won't happen again, and get stuck in.

If he could.

Traffic was heavy on the high road. It kept him slow, just as well considering. He was thirty minutes late already, a few minutes extra made no difference. He'd have to keep his helmet on, so the dressing wouldn't be seen. The first half hour was important, the greetings, the inevitable reprimand, getting moving. They'd be filling the skip for a while yet. Automatic work. The van was held at the lights, he was shivery.

He resolved to do no more than he had to. As if there was a choice.

Jack parked twenty yards up from Cromer Court. He put his helmet on. What else would be needed today? His wheel-barrow, chisels, hammer, shovel. He threw the tools in the barrow with a pair of leather gloves.

Wheel it to the man, prepare for the sad and heavy dressing down, sorry sorry sorry, spark plugs, spark plugs.

The almost empty wheelbarrow was heavier than it should be. But he couldn't afford to cry off. If he could make it till tea break, then to lunchtime, break up the day into sections. Wasn't Heidi coming over tonight for stargazing over the Flats? Centuries off. The first obstacle was the boss.

Except he wasn't around.

There was nobody at the block. The policeman had gone, the vestibule was empty, the floor plates taken away. Had Tony and Ben gone off for tea? He looked at his watch, it was eight thirty two. No way. They weren't in yet.

That was a blessing. Someone up there was looking after him.

Pity He hadn't been watching last night.

Jack must look busy, make it appear as if he'd been there and working since eight o'clock. There was a mound of rubble in the centre of the hallway, which the police had presumably sieved and taken away any evidential pieces that had survived the fire. Jack filled his wheelbarrow. That was all that was necessary. Ben and Tony couldn't know how many of these he'd carted to the skip.

He sat on a bucket, watching the doorway. The emergency lighting was off, so he was in the gloom. He would see the boss and his son before they saw him. Rest up till they came. This wasn't his job, besides he'd been hit on the head.

And burgled.

Though a strange burglary. Half asleep, with a throbbing head during the night, he hadn't reflected on it. Nor when driving in, coming up with unneeded excuses. But now, on his own, seated on the bucket, head still insisting on reminding him of its presence, things were quiet enough that he could think a little.

Someone had hit him on the head. For his keys. Clear enough. They didn't take his wallet or his phone. Just his keys to get into his flat. The burglar had known where he lived. And wasn't interested in his laptop. He could under-stand the telescope, no burglar would want to steal that. Too heavy, and who would buy it? There were no family jewels, but the burglar was obviously searching for something. Opening every cupboard, turning out every drawer.

It had to be Tony. Who else? Tony had the tin in his room and Jack had had the second one. If Tony believed Jack had it, and the stuff inside wasn't melted floor wax but had real street value, then Tony was prime suspect. He wasn't to know that Jack had given the box to Fayyad. Though might still have had it, if his friend hadn't called round.

Why leave the keys on his step? Burglars are not usually so considerate.

That was a puzzle Jack turned over, as he watched the door. He was close by flat 1 and could hear motion inside. That must be the crime scene people, measuring, dusting for prints and DNA, on hands and knees looking for traces. Fayyad had said they'd be finished with the hallway today, and they were, but would still be working in the flat.

Thinking of Fayyad gave him the answer. Jack hadn't called the police about his bashing. Wasn't going to. Nothing was taken. Just a mess to clear up. But if he'd had to smash his door in, then he would have called the cops. That would be Tony's thinking.

He had assumed Jack wouldn't call the police, not with his keys back, nothing taken, nothing provable. All he could say of his assailant was that it was someone in a hood. Most likely, Tony would have worn gloves when rummaging about the flat. And even if he hadn't been, the police wouldn't attend a burglary where nothing was taken.

They'd tell him to clear up the mess. And count himself lucky. Just a couple of bumps on the head, and empty drawers.

Someone was coming up the path. Jack rose and grabbed his spade. He threw a spadeful of rubble into the wheelbarrow as an Asian man came through the door. In his 40s maybe, short and stocky, plump around the middle, with a reef of hair around a bald dome.

Seeing Jack, he said, 'Back to work, I see.'

Jack said, 'The hall is OK, but the police are still in the flat.'

The man threw up his hands. 'I hate this dump. Drugs and low lives. I live upstairs with my wife and daughters. We want a transfer, but who'd want to do a swap and come here?'

'Are you Mr Nawaz?'

'I am,' he said, surprised. 'How come you know of me?'

'I met your wife the other day. Very nice woman.'

Mr Nawaz held up a finger. 'I hope she was veiled. I insist on that. A good Muslim woman.'

'Oh, she was. She promised me a cup of tea when your daughters were home. I was surprised she spoke to me. In a burqa and all. Not usual.'

'No, my wife does talk to people. And you seem a nice working man, so I can understand it. But not everyone round here is.' He leaned in closer. 'That man Kennedy, the man who was murdered, may he rot in hell, tried to entice my daughters into his flat, several times. I had to speak to him. I threatened to call the police.'

'What did he do?'

Mr Nawaz shrugged. 'What he always does. He hit me. I ended up in casualty. I couldn't call the police, not with my wife and daughters here, up there, so close to him, while I was out all day. He said he would rape them, one at a time. May he roast in hell's fire. My wife has to escort them to the street. After school, they phone, she comes down and escorts them in.'

'Didn't he drive a young man out of his flat?'

Mr Nawaz waved his hands in disgust. 'Poor Amir. Forced out. And him in a wheelchair. What sort of man does that?'

'And that flat too.' Jack indicated Heidi's door.

'Oh yes, that woman. Kennedy drove out a black man. And the white woman comes. She's a flighty one. I have seen different men coming and going.' He shrugged. 'What can you do? I'm a taxi driver, I'm never going to get my own house, so I have to put up with such neighbours. Drugs, sex and now murder. What a place to bring up a family!'

'Never easy,' said Jack, wondering about Mr Nawaz's opinion of Heidi. An exaggeration, surely.

'I must go up. Have some food and a rest. I've been out all night, as far as Heathrow.'

'Nice talking to you,' said Jack.

'And you, young man. Your name is?'

'Jack.'

He laughed, waving a hand in recognition. 'I saw your van. Is that you, Jack of All Trades?'

'That's me.'

'Pleased to meet you.' He put out his hand. Jack took off a leather glove and shook the offered hand. 'But I'll be glad when you're gone. Nothing personal, if you take my meaning.' He laughed.

'I understand,' said Jack. 'We make a lot of noise and a mess. And you obviously want your stairs back.'

'I feel like a burglar every time I go up that fire escape. Keep up the good work.'

He gave a wave and walked on. Jack watched him go through the garden door. And looked at the time. Ten past nine. Where were Ben and Tony?

Not that he minded them not being here. He sat back on the bucket. He was a little less groggy but not up to work mode. But why bother, if the boss isn't in? Jack had had no breakfast, and was feeling peckish. And knew that for a good sign. Illness has no appetite.

Dare he sneak off for breakfast? A quickie. He could come up with some tale. How he'd got here at seven thirty. Would that wash? How could they disprove it? He stuck the shovel in the wheelbarrow and headed out the front door.

Chapter 27

At the Forest Café, he had a cautious snack: two slices of toast and a coffee. He over sugared the coffee; energy, if bad for the teeth, as Alison would add. Jack munched slowly and sipped. A little comfort. He was still a little foggy, though the double vision had gone. He closed one eye. That was OK. Then the other, slightly foggy. Rest in the warm. He was getting paid for it. Though it was one thing the boss not being in, but his son too. But then he'd seen how Ben cosseted Tony, and how he was despised for it.

Tony wanted the tin Jack had found. He'd hit him on the head to get his house keys and searched the flat. And that black guy Sol was after it, who played that strange game on the fixed odds betting terminal. It had to be connected. The tins had been in the cleaning cupboard. Someone was using it as a hidey-hole. He'd bet on Kennedy Gerrard who would have no trouble getting the key with his strong arm practices.

Kennedy lived in flat 1, Heidi in flat 2. There were two more floors, so four more flats. The Nawaz family in one, there was Sol and whoever he lived with. There'd been that old West Indian guy. Was he Sol's relative or someone else's? Two flats on the top floor, one Kennedy had emptied and would soon have tenanted no doubt, if his plans hadn't been interrupted.

Of the six flats, Kennedy had taken over three of them. One he lived in, Heidi opposite, and the third up top. In a year, he'd have had the block.

Jack had finished his tea and toast. He'd best get back, father and son might be wondering where he was. He paid up and walked back, honing his excuse. He'd started early, so took an early breakfast.

But the excuse wasn't needed. Ben and Tony still weren't in. Fine by him. Doing nothing normally bored him, but not today with his head. And so he sat on the bucket, watching the door. It was Tony's fault, Ben's son, that Jack wasn't fit for work today, so his skiving was family payback. Except it was Ben's job. And he wasn't responsible for what his son did after hours.

Someone was coming in from the garden. Jack rose and put a shovelful of debris in the wheelbarrow. It was Sol. He approached and stopped by Jack, obviously working out what to say. The same yellow Judge Dredd t-shirt, or did he have a stack of them, though it was grubby enough to be the same. His dreadlocks languid, an air of untidiness as if he'd had little sleep.

Join the club.

Shuffling awkwardly, Sol had hands in pockets, biting his lip. Jack said nothing, stretching his legs out on the bucket, waiting for him.

Sol stood over him, looking him over. Jack looked back, giving the youngster no help.

At last, Sol said, 'You followed me into the betting office.'

'When?' said Jack as if he had no memory of it.

'Yesterday. AttaBet. Didn't you?'

'Ah, then,' said Jack. 'I went in to put on a bet.'

'I never seen you in there before. It's a black hangout.'

'It's open to anyone,' said Jack. 'I just walked up the high road and went for that one. There's no law against it.'

'You followed me. How come?'

He was picking at a spot on his face. Jack was looking at his trainers. They were fancy Adidas.

'You had a lot of money,' said Jack.

The young man shrugged. 'I won it.'

'And were giving it back again.'

'There ain't no law. You just said so.'

Jack smiled. There was no point antagonising Sol. He wouldn't get anything out of him that way. Already he'd confirmed he was a regular at the betting office.

'I used to go on those machines,' he said. 'Took all my money.' He didn't, they hadn't.

'I got a system.'

'Just bet on number 2.'

'You were looking! You were spying on me.' He frowned, accusatory.

'I couldn't see what you were doing,' said Jack, 'but this guy next to me said you came in regularly with a lot of cash and just betted on one number. A weird thing to do.'

Sol shrugged. 'So I'm weird.'

'The money was hot,' said Jack. 'Stolen or drugs. You lose 3% then get a voucher for the 97%. And get the woman at the desk to pay it into your bank account.'

'You got it all sussed, ain't you?'

'Not all.' Jack splayed his hands. 'But what's it to me? It's a free country.'

'No, it's not. Everything has to be paid for.'

'You're a sharp young fellow.'

'I learned. Had to. I live with my uncle, I'm his carer. I know about money. Without it you starve.'

'Where's your mum?'

'Mitzi is in Nigeria. She left a week ago with a man.'

'Did she get there?'

'I don't know. I ain't a spy.'

'I'd be concerned about Mitzi,' said Jack. 'Especially with a man murdered.'

'She ain't dead. She's in Nigeria.'

'How do you know?'

'I got contacts.'

'So you're not just a carer.'

He gave Jack a broad smile. 'I got sidelines.'

'Best to be flexible.'

Sol walked round the heap of rubble.

He said, 'There was two tins here. You didn't see them?'

'What was in them?'

'Stuff.'

'Like screws or washers?'

'Don't act smart. You know. I know you know.'

He changed tack, while Sol was being talkative. 'Tell you something else I know. The Nawaz family don't like you.'

'They live opposite me. I never touched their girls. Kids. Don't like my mum, Mitzi. They complain about my music. And I smoke weed. They're prejudiced.'

'Your uncle that old West Indian guy?'

'No, no. Don't you know nothing? We're African. That guy, him and his old lady, they're Jamaican. All bible. End of the world screamers. Repent, get on your knees, son. Lick the earth, you're so full of sin.'

Jack smiled. 'Too late for some of us.'

'I got a reservation in Hell. A full suite,' said Sol. 'Gotta go. Knocker needs his prescription. Or he'll moan all night. Stay cool.'

He headed away.

Jack looked at his watch, ten fifteen. And still no Ben and Tony. What was going on? A family fight. Could well be; he'd witnessed them at it yesterday. Whatever Ben did for Tony wasn't enough. He rose and massaged his backside; buckets don't make the softest seats. Lack of sleep was catching up on him. He went to the door for fresh air. The sky was cloudy, some blue patches. Might be OK for his telescope tonight. That's if he was in any state. He'd tell Ben he'd been in over two hours, and working like a Trojan. Who was to say otherwise?

Jack went in, and sat on the bucket. He was about to take off his helmet and massage his head, when Ben and Tony came onto the path. Jack rose and took up the shovel and for their benefit heaved a load into the wheelbarrow.

'Sorry, sorry, Jack,' exclaimed Ben as he came into the hall. 'Unfortunate delay. The stairs were supposed to come today. I been on the phone the last hour and a half. Now it's tomorrow. All hassle. You been busy?'

'Non-stop. Wondering whether I'd get any company. I don't know how many wheelbarrows I've filled.'

'You're a brick, mate. I hate to leave a bloke on his own. But you know, problems happen. That's the building game. You think you got it all covered, and something comes out the blue. Tell you what, why don't you go for tea. Don't rush back. Take half an hour.'

'I could do with it,' said Jack. 'Hungry work, this.'

'Thanks for sweating on your own.'

Tony hadn't said a word, sullen, watching Jack closely.

'See you in half an hour,' he said.

And left father and son.

Chapter 28

Jack had beans on toast with a mug of tea. And was finding it hard work. Faz behind the counter had remarked on his second visit within half an hour. Jack had wondered about the wisdom of coming in, if it might get back to Ben.

'I like the company,' he said.

Not untrue. He'd thought of buying a paper but with his foggy head, it wouldn't be worth the money. It was mid morning, the clientele mostly workers on tea break. A Polish gang were arguing in a corner. Jack recognised one of them, though not enough to sit with them and force them to speak English. The air was full of chips and acrid sausages. The café was cheap, cholesterol heavy. He'd considered going home; he had enough time. But remembered the mess of the burglary. And couldn't face it.

Two tea breaks, Ben thanking him, Jack couldn't help smiling. Wiping it away as Tony sat down opposite.

'Taking it easy today?' said Jack.

Tony smiled. He had a missing tooth on the upper right. Jack wondered who'd knocked it out.

'Surprised to see you,' he said.

'Why's that?' said Jack innocently.

'I heard you got a bash on the head. And got burgled.'

All the confirmation Jack needed. He hadn't told anyone about the burglary.

'You're a bastard,' he said.

Tony shrugged. 'I've been called worse.'

'What d'you want?'

'You know.'

Tony could've been called handsome, with his smooth cheeks and light brown hair. Mixed with vinegar in Jack's ken. He was muscular, the legacy of weight training in the nick, no doubt. Pushy, Jack knew the type. It never paid to back down.

'Like the box under your mattress?' he said.

Tony banged a fist into his palm, making it do for Jack's face.

'I knew you'd been in there,' he said.

'I kept it tidy,' said Jack. 'Which is more than you did.'

'I thought of taking your laptop. Family pictures and all.'

'What stopped you? Kindness?'

'I figured you wouldn't report it if nothing was missing.'

So Jack had been right. A small consolation for a smack on the head.

He said, 'There were more than two tins, weren't there? They were the tail end.'

'Who told you?'

From Tony's fierce look, he knew he'd hit home.

'Who?' he demanded.

'A woman.' Drawing it out of the blue, there being a narrow choice of sexes.

'One who came to see you last night?'

Jack realised he'd picked wrong, fingering Heidi.

'A black woman,' he said. 'With gold earrings.' Adding as an afterthought, 'in a massage parlour.'

It was a hopeless lie. He shouldn't have started.

Tony waved a vehement finger. 'I want that tin. Where is it?'

'The cops have it.'

'I don't believe you.'

'Then ask for Detective Sergeant Fayyad Kamani at the desk of Forest Gate Police Station. Sorry, I didn't get a receipt.'

Tony was breathing heavily, attempting to sort fact from fiction. Neither spoke for a while, daring the other to look away.

'You're a fool,' said Tony. 'Just like my old man. You find a tin worth thousands and you hand it in. You make me sick. Who does it help? One day you'll be fifty, your back gone. And you'll still be shovelling sand into wheelbarrows.'

'Go to the cops and claim it's yours,' said Jack. 'Tell them it has sentimental value. I'm sure they'll hand it over.'

Tony stood up and picked up the plate of beans on toast and slammed it at Jack. Jack ducked, and the plate hit the wall, shattering, scattering beans and sauce across the café, spots landing on Jack's face.

Tony strode out, daring anyone to stop him.

Chapter 29

Jack apologised for the mess in the café, which was being cleared up when he came out of the toilet, having washed his face.

Faz told him Tony was banned.

'He's trouble.'

Jack agreed. And Dino offered Jack another plate of beans, but Jack had been having trouble eating a second breakfast. So he apologised again and turned down the grub. He felt responsible for Tony's action. This was his regular café. He hated his part in bringing Tony in.

He left, holding back another apology. It wasn't him who'd thrown the beans.

Back at the site, the door was wide open, held back with rubble. Ben had brought in his wheelbarrow and was loading it up.

'Where'd you go?' said Ben.

'Forest Café.'

'Thought you would. They make a decent breakfast.'

Jack picked up a shovel and attacked the heap. With Ben here, he'd have to do some work, though his head rebelled with each lift.

'Did you see Tony?' said Ben. 'He went there for a bite.'

Jack hesitated, but thought what the hell. It'd come out anyway.

'He and I had a row in the café.'

Ben stopped mid shovelling. 'Over what?'

'Tony hit me on the head last night.' Jack took off his helmet and showed the dressing. 'On the railway bridge. He came at me from behind. He's admitted it.'

'Hit you on the head?'

'Yes. I was in casualty for four hours.'

'Hit you on the head?' He was staring at the dressing as if to burn it away. 'He's got a temper, Tony has, but he wouldn't hit you. Not my boy. He wouldn't.'

'He thinks I've got something of his. A box I found. But I gave it to the cops. He doesn't believe me.'

'What's in the box?'

'Drugs. Must be. Worth enough to make him hit me on the head.'

'He's a fool. I've let him get away with too much. Where is he now?'

'Don't know. Don't care.'

Ben let out a yell. 'He's at the betting office! He's banned, the condition of his bail. I don't believe it.' His hands pummelled his helmeted head.

Jack continued shovelling. Tony could break bail conditions any day of the week, and he'd dance a jig when the cops picked him up.

'I've got to stop him,' exclaimed Ben. 'Sorry to leave you, but he mustn't break his bail conditions... He's headstrong. He doesn't mean it. He doesn't think.' Ben strode out. 'I'll see you all right, Jack.'

And he was out the hallway and pacing away down the path. Jack watched him go onto the street and turn from view. Satisfied that he too was out of view, Jack laid the shovel in the wheelbarrow and sat down on the bucket. He had the remnant of a headache, and was fatigued, the world at a distance as if he were a guest, unsure whether to stay or go.

He hoped he'd taken any heat off Heidi in his set to with Tony. It had been stupid saying it was a woman who had told him there were other tins. It was a guess, hazarding that two had been the remnant of a hoard. How many had there been, who had them now?

Tony, Sol? Who knows?

A middle aged Asian man came out of Heidi's flat, closing the door carefully. He was smartly dressed in a shiny leather jacket and chiselled toed black shoes.

Surprised at his exit, Jack said, 'Is Heidi in?'

'You mean Miss Whiplash?'

He almost said 'who?' but held back. An inkling of something not right.

'Yes,' said Jack, going with the tale. 'I hear she's hot.'

'Man!' He was rubbing his hands, 'the best. I don't know why she works from this hole. If she got herself a decent flat, she could make twice the money.' He grinned and nudged Jack. 'My wife thinks I've been to the gym.'

'I'm sure you had a good workout,' said Jack.

The man laughed. 'You should've seen my bench press.' He couldn't stop chuckling, tapping Jack on the shoulder as if they were old pals. 'My clean and jerk,' he managed to add in his paroxysm. 'A hole in one,' he exclaimed, mixing metaphors. 'A birdie, an eagle, an albatross!'

'I'm glad you weren't below par,' joined in Jack. 'And didn't lose your ball in a bunker.'

The man was clutching his stomach in pained laughter.

'Oh my, oh yes, we ended up in the rough.'

He staggered off waving, like a drunk leaving a jolly party.

'I hit it for six, straight across the boundary. A hat trick! A googly, a penalty shoot out!'

The sport metaphors might have amused Jack if he'd been talking of a stranger. Heidi had told him she had an early shift at the hospital. It was the reason she gave for leaving at nine thirty last night.

Miss Whiplash.

He went outside to the rectangle of buzzers, hardly necessary as he could have knocked on her flat door, but out of formality, he pressed the bell of flat 2.

'Hello. Who's there?' answered the tinny speaker.

Could be her, could be someone else.

'I'm here for Miss Whiplash.' He husked his voice, to make it less recognizable.

'You're early.'

'I couldn't wait.'

'Come in then.'

Jack went round the mound of rubble and wheelbarrows to her door. He adjusted his helmet, and stuck his thumb over the spy hole.

'Who's there?' came a female voice, probably Heidi, maybe not.

'Jack,' he said, knowing he'd be revealed soon enough.

There was no reply for a few seconds. He wondered what he was letting himself in for. Was it Heidi or Miss Whiplash, whoever she might be?

'Let me see you.'

Jack took his thumb off the spy hole. And stood stock still, knowing she could see his fish-eyed face and yellow helmet. Not a flattering way to be viewed, but he wasn't out to flatter or fix a sink.

A bolt was pulled, a lock turned. The door opened.

And there was Heidi, her face creamy and thick with make-up, in an orange wig that lapped her shoulders. She was wearing a short, bright green dressing gown, her legs bare, down to ornate leather boots with spurs. Lying on the floor was a lasso made from deep yellow rope.

She saw him looking and kicked the rope aside.

'What do you want?' she said.

There was no hint of warmth, or any of the feeling of yesterday. This was Heidi, before she'd met him, in a parallel universe.

'You're not a nurse,' he said, realising its stupidity as he said it.

'Do I look it?'

'Not today.'

'I was going to text you. This evening is cancelled.'

Jack nodded, unable to keep his eyes off her heavily made up face, the garish orange wig. 'I can see things have changed. You seemed to like me yesterday.'

She shrugged. 'It's my job to like men.'

'Thank you for the freebie,' he said with no feeling of gratitude. 'I'm sure you don't often give them.'

'That was a one-off.'

Her lips were the same orange shade as her hair. Her eye shadow was dark blue, her scent he recognised from yesterday. He wondered what she was wearing under the dressing gown. Not much, clearly.

'Why?' he said.

'I have a client coming in ten minutes,' she said, ignoring his question. 'I must get ready.'

'You haven't been working the last couple of days…'

'What! With all those cops around? How could I?'

He had a disturbing thought. Anything could be true. Or false.

'You contacted Tony after I saw you home,' he said.

She shrugged.

'Your coming to my place,' he said, churning furiously, 'was to get the box from me.' A sudden thought. 'The vacuum cleaning!'

She smiled.

He'd been lying back in bed, pleasantly weary after sex, she vacuuming naked in the sitting room. All so she could look round the flat. Under the sofa, the table, sideboard, every corner, the kitchen. But had not found the box, so she'd called Tony to do a more thorough search.

'Tony and I had a chat in Forest Café half an hour ago,' he said. 'I told him I knew there were ten boxes. Said you told me.'

'Liar!' she exclaimed.

'He said you are partners.' In what, he had only a hint. 'Fifty fifty. Kennedy dead. Finders keepers.'

She sucked a knuckle, considering what her partner may have admitted. Tony was a lit firecracker. Not the soundest associate.

'I persuaded him to leave your keys on the step,' she said.

'Do you want a tip?'

She sighed, and took a breath. 'I have a client coming and I must get ready, Jack. So enough chit chat. You get the picture. Or some of it. But let me warn you. Don't meddle. There are dangerous people involved. And you're a nice guy. I did enjoy our dinner, but sex is work. I do it to earn my keep, not for pleasure.'

'Kennedy was your pimp.'

'Too close a relationship,' she said, indicating the door opposite. 'He set me up here, held me.'

'You're free now.'

'I have to move house. That much is true.'

'And little else,' he said. She had played him along. A nurse, however could he have believed her? A thought struck him. 'Who has the other room in your place?'

'I told you not to meddle.'

'Is it Mitzi?'

'Leave it, Jack. I must go.'

She tried to push the door shut but his foot was over the step.

'I hear she ran off with a Nigerian,' he hissed.

'So why are you asking me?'

His foot was between the door and the post. She pushed hard against it, grimacing.

'Who else are you in with?' he said, holding his foot firmly over the doorstep.

Suddenly, she opened the door a little way, he rocked forward in surprise as the pressure came off. She came in quickly and kneed him in the groin. With a yell, Jack backed off, clutching himself.

'Sorry, Jack, but you asked for it.'

Chapter 30

For the next few minutes he crouched over, wincing as he stomped about. At last, ceasing his turkey shuffle, he leaned against the wall. The woman at flat 2 with a face like Heidi, but with an orange wig and garish lips, wasn't coming out tonight with him and his telescope. Or on any other night. She was in cahoots with Tony. They had boxes and boxes. How many? Pick a number.

He straightened up when a crime scene operative came out of flat 1. She was carrying a large cardboard box with a lid, which she had to put down to close the door, enabling Jack to see inside the flat for a few seconds. There were two others, indeterminate sex, dressed as she was, head to foot in white paper suits, with plastic gloves, masks and overshoes, crawling on the floor.

The woman shut the door and picked up the cardboard box.

'You finishing today?' he managed to say.

'Probably this afternoon.' She peered at him closely. 'You all right?'

'I banged my knee,' he said. 'Be fine in a minute or two.'

He rubbed it to emphasise the pain of it.

'Don't kill yourself,' she said with a brief smile. 'You don't get paid enough.'

And left him.

He watched her go down the path, arms clutched round the big box. Full of bits and pieces, he surmised, that might help the police. And wryly thought the knee in the groin had been apt. Heidi had been a complete act. A first date is always something of an act. Expected. Best behaviour, cleaned and scrubbed, trying to be what the other wants. But not a thorough going con.

Her plan had been to search his flat. The coldness of it, the calculation. Heidi had gone to bed with him, no pressure. But not out of any desire, simply to exhaust him, so she could rummage. He'd been lying back, relaxed, while she vacuumed, doubtless looking in cupboards and drawers as the machine roared.

The rejection hurt. He was never in the running. Sex was work for Heidi. She could scream for England, but was as phony as a three pound note. As was the nurse palaver, another avatar, along with Miss Whiplash and whoever else filled the costume trunk. And Mitzi too. Did they do two-somes as harlequins or randy lesbians, pimped by the impresario Kennedy?

It would be cheap stuff, ridiculous as a porn movie designed to get a housewife to take her clothes off for the plumber. Not believable, unless for sex, which made the fantasy work like a belief in Santa Claus, which could be another costume in the box.

Actors to small audiences. Though she had persuaded Tony to leave the keys on the step. A bash on the head, a flat turned upside down, were acceptable. But she'd balked at leaving him out in the cold.

Not quite the whore with the heart of gold. A single cell of goodness.

Jack went outside, more or less recovered from the knee in the groin. He gazed down the road to see if Ben was on the way back, with errant son in tow. But couldn't see them. And wondered about Heidi's next punter who was due shortly. Or so she'd said. Then again, credibility was not her strong suit. There was no one around. Though a car might turn up with a pumped up male aching to play a sick patient for the randy nurse. Or the horse for Miss Whiplash.

He went inside, massaging his groin. Stop. Enough. Anyone could come along. No damage done down there. Leave it. He could walk upright and maybe even do some work.

From the garden door came Mr Nawaz in a brown leather jacket, the garment of the day it seemed.

Jack said, 'Out in the cab?'

Mr Nawaz straightened his jacket. 'I have a little business with the woman downstairs.' He came in closer. 'My wife's birthday is coming up, you know. I want to ask Miss Miles what one might buy her. Not too fancy, you know. But something to spice things up, between man and wife.'

'I'm sure Heidi can help you.'

'You know her?'

'I fixed her sink the other day.' He'd admit nothing more intimate.

'A Jack of all trades you truly are.'

Mr Nawaz went to the door. Jack play acted a little shovelling, curious about Heidi in costume. The door opened, but she stood well back, so he was unable to see her, though a blast of scent issued, the same as last night's. And Mr Nawaz was quickly inside and the door shut.

His headache had returned. He needed some painkillers. The air in the hall was fuzzy, the mock shovelling had affected something. Jack went out in the open air. Breathe. Take in the air, feel each breath going in. It was a technique taught at Alcohol Halt. Be in the moment. Don't think about what's going on in flat 2. Breathe. Or think if you must, but feel, observe your body and your mind's fantasies.

After a minute or so, he went back inside. He should do some work. He had a face mask in his overall pocket. It was grubby but would do. He didn't want to go out to the van for a clean one. Besides, he wasn't going to work hard. Just enough to take his mind off things. At least he had no date to worry about tonight. He'd go to bed early. But no, the flat! The mess of it.

Awaiting his return.

Jack filled a wheelbarrow, shovel by deliberate shovelful. Normally he'd be working three times as fast, especially if working for himself, but his head, his heart too it should be added, slackened the body.

What had Tony said to him earlier? You'll be fifty with a broken back and still shovelling sand. Jack grimaced, feeling that he would get there much sooner at this rate.

A young Asian man was coming up the path on crutches. Another for Miss Whiplash? Perhaps the Nurse. She has them all, young and old, able bodied and disabled. An equal opportunities worker.

'Hello,' said the young man, coming into the hall. He was breathless, dressed in denim jacket and jeans, his black hair was short and tidy. He was looking about the hall. 'I heard there was a fire.'

'Kids,' said Jack. 'But worse than fire in there.' He pointed out flat 1. 'Murder.'

'I heard,' he said. 'It's my flat. Mrs Nawaz phoned my mother. I've come to have a look at it. See what condition it's in.'

Jack apologised silently for assuming the young man was Heidi's client. And said, 'I'm afraid the crime scene people are in there.'

'That's a nuisance. I've come all the way from East Ham. Got a taxi even.'

'You must be the young man Kennedy Gerrard forced out?'

'That monster. Don't remind me. I shouldn't say it, but I don't care who knows it, I am glad he's dead.' He stumbled on his crutches, agitated by his memories. 'I need some-where to sit down. No steps here? I thought I could get here without my wheelchair. I have good days and bad days. I must sit or I'll collapse.'

He was leaning against the wall, gasping, eyes all but closed. Jack thought rapidly, a chair was needed. Heidi wasn't an option. Busy, and he'd had more than enough of her.

He knocked on flat 1.

The door was opened promptly by a man in crime scene gear.

He said, 'I am sorry, this is a crime scene.' And then recognised him. 'Oh, you're the builder. What do you want? We're working.'

'Sorry to disturb you,' said Jack. 'But this young man...' He indicated him gasping against the wall, beginning to slip down. 'It's his flat. And he really needs a chair.'

The investigator bit his lip. 'Shouldn't. But we're almost done. OK. Wait a mo.'

He went in and Jack crossed to the young man. He put his hands under the young man's armpits and gently raised him against the wall. Jack could feel the man's legs had given up.

'I thought I was all right today,' he said. 'But coming here brings it all back. Last year. That horrible man.'

'I understand,' said Jack. 'No one has a good word to say for him.'

The crime scene operative came out with a wooden chair.

'This one's clean,' he said, 'been gone over twice for fin-gerprints, DNA and any other traces. Please sit down.'

Jack helped him into the chair.

'Thank you so much,' said the young man, breathing heavily, but beginning to relax now he was seated. 'I am sorry to be so much trouble.'

'I'll get you some tea,' said the operative. He went back into the flat.

'He beat me up. Kennedy,' said the young man. 'Several times. Smashed the flat. I have flashbacks. I was fine this morning. Thought, yes, I'll use my crutches. I like to use them as much as I can. But being here, all the energy has been sucked out of me.'

The operative came out with a thermos.

'No sugar, I'm afraid.'

'That's fine.'

He poured him a cup of tea in the thermos mug.

'Here. Keep the flask.' To Jack he said, 'Drop it back in.'

'Sure.'

'Glad I could help. Must do my bit or they'll have a go at me.' The operative went inside and closed the door.

The young man sipped the tea.

'I hate being any trouble,' he said. 'That's what was awful about going back home. I had my own flat here. I was independent, I'm taking a Masters in Artificial Intelligence at the University of East London. And then Gerrard came.'

'He's gone now,' said Jack. 'And not coming back. That's your flat again.'

'It'll be full of his stuff.'

'The Council will clear it for you. Contact them.'

'Thank you for your help. I don't know your name. How rude of me, I haven't introduced myself. I'm Amir Noor.'

'I'm Jack Bell. Pleased to meet you.'

They shook hands.

'I'm stopping you working,' said Amir.

Jack smiled. 'You're not. I'm doing as little as possible.' He raised his helmet showing the dressing. 'The boss's son hit me on the head, so I'm skiving. Well, hardly. I can't do much, but had to come into work. I need the money.'

'Two invalids,' said Amir. 'I've got a battery operated wheelchair. Fine for going to the local shops, but it's a pain going anywhere longer, hiring special taxis. I thought I'd manage on crutches. Stupid of me. I must stop complaining. I've a chair and a cup of tea.'

'Tell me about this flat,' said Jack. He pointed out Heidi's place. 'Who lived there in your time?'

'There was a West Indian man living there, nice guy, Mr Greene, but Kennedy cleared him off. He put two prostitutes in, just before he drove me out. Heidi, that's her name, one of the women, and there was Mitzi, a mixed race woman. They dressed up for clients. It was so funny. I've seen them open the door, Heidi as a nurse. Mitzi, I saw dressed as a waitress in a short skirt, hardly longer than a belt.' A sudden thought. 'Mitzi actually lives upstairs. With her son and brother. This is where she worked.'

There was a car hooter from outside, and then another.

'That's my taxi. I said I'd only be quarter of an hour.'

'I'll tell him you're here. And you might be a bit slow,' said Jack.

He went out and down the path. The cab had managed to pull in close by. Jack went to the driver.

'He's coming,' he said. 'But taking his time, he's had a shock.'

'Wasn't there a murder here?'

The cabbie was Middle Eastern, possibly Turkish.

'There was,' said Jack.

'Not surprised. I've brought guys here to pick up drugs. They never said it was drugs. But they'd be ten minutes and come out beaming and talkative. Through the mirror, I'd see 'em splitting the gear in the back seat. There's a couple of working girls too. I've brought punters here.' He laughed. 'Run a taxi, learn about life.'

'I've seen a few sights myself,' said Jack. 'I'll see how he's getting on.'

Amir was on the path, already exhausted from the short walk. Jack went inside and brought out the chair.

Halfway down the path, Amir took a break.

'Do you do decorations, Jack?'

'I do.'

'I'd like the flat decorated. Do you want the job?'

'Pleased to take it on. But you've got to get it cleared first.'

'I'll get that sorted when I get home. I'll crowdfund the decorating. The Mosque will help out too.'

He rose and walked on a little. Taking several breaks, he got to the cab. The driver had the door open for him and Amir sank into the seat. Jack stayed to wave him off. No sign of Ben or his son down the road.

Chapter 31

'You're banned.'

It was the blonde manager in her grey monogrammed uniform, hands on hips to emphasise that he wasn't staying.

'I just got a little business,' said Tony. 'No trouble. I got to talk to this bloke, then I'll be off.'

'You're banned. Out now, or I call the police.'

She had taken out her phone, daring him. But it only incensed Tony. A woman! He held his ground, staring at her. She'd back down all right. A commentary was running on the TV, horses and riders being identified in the paddock. The mostly black men had put down their pencils and papers. The one busy punter was an older man on a fixed odds machine. His roulette numbers couldn't wait or his luck would run out.

'One minute,' said Tony. 'Just turn your back, sweetheart. One minute.'

The manager pushed three numbers on her phone.

A big black man came forward. 'I'll deal with this, Jane. No need for the cops.'

She brought down her phone.

'Hiya, Boz,' said Tony putting out a hand in affected affability. 'It's the business I spoke to you about.'

Boz ignored the proffered hand. He was in a green t-shirt and jeans, with a thick woolly hat with a bobble the size of a fist. Every day, bar Sunday, he was at Atherton gym pumping iron. In the light heavy weight division, he held the East London record for clean and jerk.

Boz poked Tony in the chest with a finger. 'You don't cause trouble here, man. You're banned.'

'I only need a minute.'

'Not here,' said Boz. 'The lady says out, I say out.'

He pushed Tony with the flat of his hand.

'Don't get rough,' said Tony, stumbling back.

'We don't want the law coming round. Get me? I'll talk to you outside.'

He brusquely turned Tony about, ushering him forward like a troublemaker at a nightclub.

'I'm going, I'm going, quit the pushing. I got other options, you know.'

'Outside,' said Boz.

Once on the high street, Boz hooked his arm in Tony's. Not a friendly gesture, tugging him along.

A bus crawled past, a row of cars behind. A woman in a rush scampered across the road, setting off hooting.

'You're banned,' said Boz. 'You stay out of AttaBet. It's our place. We do business there. You just bring cops. We don't want trouble. Get me?'

'Yeh. I just wanted to tell you, I got the stuff.'

'Enough. Don't tell the street. Round the corner.'

Boz directed him down the side road. At the end was a brick cylinder, about 30 feet high and 50 across, a ventilation shaft for the high speed trains to Europe.

Pushing Tony against a wall, Boz said, 'How much you got?'

'Eleven boxes.'

'I thought you said twelve.'

'One got lost.'

'How come?'

'Someone filched it. I'm dealing with it.'

'We could deal with it.'

'I'm on top of it.'

'I bet you are,' said Boz. 'Let's have a sniff.'

Tony took out a wrap of silver foil and handed it to him. Boz unwrapped it and sniffed it several times, like a wine connoisseur testing the bouquet. He crumbled it in his fingers and sniffed some more.

'This is OK,' he said. 'I'm not giving a price till I see it all.'

'Gimme an idea.'

'Five to ten.'

'I can get twelve.'

'Then get yourself twelve.'

'If you don't want to deal...' said Tony, making as if to leave, but he wanted the sample back.

'Ten max,' said Boz. He blew a raspberry. 'I mean max. I've calls to make. I'll contact you where and when. Bring it all, and no funny business. Or you're dead.'

'I'm straight,' said Tony. 'All I want is a fair deal.'

'Shake.'

They shook. Boz squeezed hard. Tony squeezed back but couldn't compete with the weightlifter's grip.

Chapter 32

A chair made easier sitting than a bucket. It had come from Kennedy's place but CSI had no further use for it. They'd checked it for traces: fingerprints, blood spots, DNA, anything a body exudes. By all accounts, it had been a busy flat when Kennedy was alive, visited by assorted small dealers, impromptu parties, underage girls. Plenty to enrage Mr Nawaz who was still busy at number 2.

Enquiring about presents for his wife.

Amir had offered him the work doing up his flat. Fine, but that would be weeks away. The flat had to be emptied first. He knew from experience that could take ages. The Council had to contact relatives about the furniture and personal pieces filling the place. Or maybe not, as Kennedy had no right to be there. But there might be some valuable gear. Kennedy made money.

Amir had left him a phone number. He would advise him to get in as soon as he could and take his pick of what was going. He deserved it.

Jack looked at his watch. Time for lunch. Not that he was hungry. He'd had two breakfasts, well, one and a half. And had done next to no work. He could go home for half an hour. Oh no, he recalled the chaos that awaited.

He was considering what to do, when Mr Nawaz came out in a blast of scent as the door of flat 2 opened. The odour had been pleasant last night, but that was a dab, and this was a tidal wave. Nawaz glanced at him guiltily, a half smile, but said nothing and scuttled out of the hallway. Jack surmised he'd have to work a full day to pay for his pleasure. He wondered how often he visited. Did his wife suspect?

Heidi was at the door of her flat in a long paisley dressing gown. She had on the orange wig, her thick make-up smudged. She was holding the yellow lasso. Seeing it was only Jack, she tore off the wig, and threw it on the floor in a corner with the lasso.

'That is so hot,' she exclaimed, 'especially this weather. Do you want a cup of tea?'

Jack was surprised at the request.

'It won't be poisoned?'

'You're not a rat,' she said, and indicated with her head. 'Come in.'

He put the chair against the wall and considered. He wasn't a punter or lover. Hardly a friend. Though she was making a gesture. What did she want to know?

He was almost knocked out as the scent hit him in her hallway.

'You must buy that perfume by the bucket,' he exclaimed, entering the kitchen.

'I don't smell it anymore,' she said, leading him into the kitchen. 'It's not cheap. I try not to be.'

'Your brand,' he said.

'Marketing is marketing,' she said. 'Don't try to compete with the lowest price.'

He sat on a stool at the table. Last time he'd been here was to fix the sink.

'What do you do with the lasso?' He was intrigued, a little excited at the possibilities.

'Games,' she said. 'Silly games. I throw a good rope.'

'I'm surprised you stay in Forest Gate,' he said. 'You're more upmarket.'

She smiled, pleased by the flattery.

'I never aimed to stay,' she said. 'But Kennedy kept me here. Held me in his iron grip.'

She had filled the kettle and turned it on.

'And Mitzi too?'

'The same.' She was rinsing the teapot. 'When you've been beaten up by Kennedy, you work hard to avoid it happening again. If you are going to do a runner, you must plan it to a T.'

'Did Mitzi plan it?'

'I don't know. Wise girl, she didn't tell me, thinking I might go running off to Kennedy. Or he'd have forced it out of me. She had this regular punter, Peto, a Nigerian, at least he said he was. You can be what you like here. But he had a lot of cash, gold rings, expensive suits and handmade shoes. Anyway, about a week ago, they went to the casino in Stratford. She OK'd it with Kennedy. They'd gone before. She'd dressed up to the nines to make Peto look grand, big spender, smart woman on his arm. He gave her gambling money for the tables. But this time, she didn't come back. And I got a beating up for being in on it.'

'But you weren't.'

'Kennedy said I must have known.' She sat down opposite Jack. She looked dowdy, the wig off, streaked make-up, lines at the edge of her eyes. He wondered how old she was. There was no point asking; she was selective with the truth.

'Mitzi didn't live here,' he said. 'Did she?'

'No, she lived upstairs with her son and brother. She used the room here for work.'

'Kennedy had half the block. Three of the six flats.'

'I suspect he'd have had the lot in another year. Total control. That was the way he worked.'

'He lived in flat 1, you here, flat 2,' said Jack, trying to keep tabs on who was where. 'But he also had flat 6 up top. Did he have plans for it?'

'None that he told me.'

'How long has it been empty?'

'Six months.'

'I wonder why.'

'Me too,' she said. 'He could've put some girls in. But he left it. Must be a reason. Toast?'

'No thanks. The last piece was thrown at me by your partner.'

'Partner?' She was puzzled for an instant. 'Oh, you mean Tony.'

'He threw it at me, plate and all, in the Forest Café this morning.'

'Ah.' She nodded. 'The box.'

'The one I gave to the cops.'

'I happen to believe you,' she said as she poured hot water into the teapot. 'But Tony assumes everyone is like him.'

'Not the best choice for a partner. How did it happen?'

'An accident. Well, sort of,' she reflected. 'A couple of nights ago, Tony was my punter.'

'Nurse or Miss Whiplash?'

She threw up a disparaging hand. 'Can't remember. They merge. Order them about, get them to take their clothes off. Nurse, Miss Whiplash, Cowgirl, much the same.' She paused for a second. 'Nurse. I had to take his temperature. I have a big thermometer, I stick it up the bum. It needs several readings. Anyway, I'm not telling you trade secrets. That night, we were all done, I saw him to the door, I always do that. Good manners. And Kennedy's door was open across the hall. Tony wanted to buy some stuff, I had money to give Kennedy. So we went in together, and there was

Kennedy, dead. And there were the tins stacked up. Ready to go.'

'I thought he kept them in the cleaning cupboard,' said Jack.

'These had either just been delivered, or had just been taken out ready to go. I really don't know. Does it matter?'

'Not a lot.'

'Two were still in the cupboard. We found out about them later. Or rather Tony did. And so did you.' She shrugged. 'Anyway, we'd got the bulk. We couldn't do anything about the body, so why get involved? Just take the booty. Tony suggested hiding the boxes at my place. And so there it was, instant partnership. Not the best, I agree. But you have to take your opportunities.'

'Why are you telling me this?'

'You know we have the stuff. It wouldn't take much to work out where it had come from.'

'I guessed it came from Kennedy. Every dirty job round here begins with him.'

'There you are.'

'Have you still got the boxes here?'

She laughed. 'Planning to cut me out? I deserve it. But no, the stash isn't here, it was a very temporary stopover; we knew the cops would be here soon enough.'

She poured the tea into two mugs.

'I am sorry about last night's trouble,' she added.

'You half agreed to a meal before you knew I had the box.'

'Less than half. I didn't know your address. Bit of fun.'

She passed him a mug.

'The cops came. So no punters. Tony tells me you must have the other box. Worth a thou. So I go looking for you. And find you in the Forest Café. I invite myself to dinner...'

'And I thought it was my charm.'

'They all do, Jack.' She took a sip of tea. 'While at your place, the plan was to do a search. Which meant sex, no big deal.'

'And when you found nothing, you called Tony.'

'The bash on the head was unavoidable, Jack. Sorry about the mess. Did the sex make up for it?'

'No.'

'I don't like to disappoint, but I won't be rescheduling.'

'I've gathered that. And I wouldn't accept anyway.'

'I dare say I could persuade you.' She smirked, sure of herself.

Could she, he thought. All those men, one after another, nauseating. The play acting: cowgirl, nurse, Miss Whiplash. And the aftermath of smudged make-up, the wig, the smell of the place.

Maybe she could. On a cold night.

'You're all the same. Men,' she said. 'A few shakes of the hips and you're up for it.' She took a sip of tea. 'I prefer women. Curvier, softer. They don't cheat so often.'

'Did you and Mitzi have a thing?'

'We could be honest with each other.'

'She wasn't at the end.'

'No. But I don't blame her for that. I just hope she's safe.' She rose. 'Are you sure you won't have toast?'

He relented. 'Go on, bribe me then. And maybe some cheese.'

It was lunchtime anyway.

Chapter 33

Heidi put an egg on the toast as well as cheese, and they chatted about where Heidi might live. She told him of the problem of finding a place where she could both live and work without forking out most of her wages. She'd leave flat hunting for a few days, and earn money, which she'd need for moving. It would be expensive, but at least she could keep all her earnings as Kennedy wouldn't be taking the lion's share. And Tony could sell their stash.

Jack left and actually did some work. His head had cleared while he'd been with Heidi and he was almost back to strength. Any thoughts of a relationship had gone. She was no longer the woman she'd been. But she had more or less apologised and that was the best he could expect.

Ben wasn't back, nor Tony. This was the weirdest of jobs. The boss nowhere to be seen and he, the only worker, could do what he wanted. From what Heidi had said, it was likely Tony was out wheeling and dealing. With his dad looking for him.

So be it.

Jack worked at his own pace, no one to overlook him. But he would work, it was boring sitting around, watching out for the boss. It was dogsbody work with no skill, simply getting rid of the heap of rubble in the hall. He'd fill a wheelbarrow, wheel it out to the skip by the side of the road, and empty it. If there'd been two of them, they could have lifted it over the side, but a full wheelbarrow was too heavy for one, so he had to shovel it out. Laborious and slow.

Not his problem.

With a couple of planks up the skip side, he could've run the barrow up and tipped the load out. Not recommended, though he had done it. But there were no planks, so no risking life and limb on a job that wasn't his. One that was going to be losing money. There could be no doubt about it.

Were the stairs ever coming? Not that they were ready for them. The hallway had to be cleared first.

This was a cock-up of a job.

He was filling the wheelbarrow when a woman in a black burqa came through from the garden door. He knew most of the tenants now. Had to be Mrs Nawaz, short, plump, just her eyes visible in the slit in the fabric.

'Hello,' he said.

'Did my husband go in there?' She indicated Heidi's place.

'I don't know,' he said, sensing trouble. 'I was off at lunch.'

'He came back to the flat, to get change, smelling of the whorehouse.'

'I don't know anything about it.'

'You men, always defending each other.' She shook her arms in fury. 'First there is Kennedy dragging my girls in, then this woman dragging my husband in.'

'I don't think he was dragged in,' he said, realising he was admitting too much as the words came out.

'So he did go in. And you saw, didn't you?'

'I don't want to get involved in your family affairs.'

'She's a slut.'

Jack thought, what does that make your husband?

'I don't know how many men she has in a day. And one of them my husband. Why do men need it? Am I not a good wife?'

'I'm sure you are,' he said. What else could he say?

He could feel the burn of anger through the fabric, her eyes wide as she strode about. And all at once, she was hammering on Heidi's door.

'Open up, you slut! Open up, you wicked woman!'

All the time thumping at the door, yelling. She'll break her hands, thought Jack.

'You steal the food from my daughters' mouths! You husband stealer! Open up, whore!'

Jack headed off for the skip with half a wheelbarrow, to get away from the thumping and yelling. How was Heidi reacting to the hurricane at her doorway? Halfway down the path, the tirade ceased. Jack turned; Heidi's door had opened. He couldn't see her but it must be her. And then Mrs Nawaz was in. Whether invited or she'd pushed her way through, he couldn't be sure. Some of each perhaps.

He shovelled the load into the skip, intensely curious about what was happening in the flat between the women. Mrs Nawaz was a bundle of rage, but Heidi could defend herself. A couple of days ago, she might have called in Kennedy.

Was Heidi at risk? Mrs Nawaz was in such a fury, Heidi had a knife rack in her kitchen. He dismissed the thought. Mrs Nawaz wasn't that crazy. She had two daughters.

And a husband. Suppose Heidi agreed to ban him, the taxi driver had plenty of other choices. His wife couldn't beat down every red light door in London. There would be family rows, maybe there were already. The daughters cringing in their bedroom. He remembered his own mother and father at it. His mother screaming, 'Go to that woman then!' And eventually, his father had.

When he returned to the hallway, flat 2's door was closed, but Jack could hear the yelling within. Only Mrs Nawaz. He couldn't hear Heidi who was letting her blast out.

Who did he side with? With Mrs Nawaz certainly, short on housekeeping money, expecting better of a 'good' Muslim husband. Heidi to some extent. If she didn't have him, some other working girl would. It wasn't as if she was compelling him. Though maybe she was, by just being there, sex being sex, demanding and on the doorstep. Mr Nawaz was married with two daughters, his wife utterly faithful, doing her duty by him, but he was bored with their sex life. Childrearing and time had reduced her sexual allure. There were strict limits to what she would do. Heidi offered spice, flair.

The shouting had stopped. Was Heidi making her tea? The thought amused him. She should have been a social worker. She soothed well. Perhaps it came with the job.

A middle aged black man in a baggy grey suit was at the block door, pushing one of the outside bells. Jack heard Heidi through the intercom: 'Come to flat 2, Abe.'

Jack shovelled, half watching. The man went to the door combing his thin grey hair, ignoring Jack.

The door opened, Mrs Nawaz came out. Jack wondered what the punter made of a woman in a burqa coming out of such a flat. He went in and the door closed.

'Is it sorted out, Mrs Nawaz?'

'Perhaps.' She opened her hand revealing crushed bank-notes. 'She gave me fifty pounds and said she wouldn't deal with him any more.'

'What are you going to do?'

'I don't know. I could go to his parents. I could go to the sharia court.' She was weeping. 'The shame, the shame of it. How can I tell everyone what my husband is doing?'

Jack was out of his depth. It was a marriage, and he knew advice was rarely welcomed, and across cultures too. He was neutered.

'I am so sorry,' he said.

She wiped her eyes with the back of her hand, sniffing.

'One last chance,' she said, 'and then if that doesn't work, I will go to sharia court.'

Jack thought, and if that fails too? But kept it to himself, knowing that in some eyes divorce was a greater sin than a husband visiting prostitutes.

'The money he should spend on his family, goes to this lady,' she went on, the money in her fist shaking as she punched out her argument. 'OK, she says no more, but there are plenty of ladies on Green Street and the Romford Road.' She stopped, and shook her head. 'Please don't repeat this. It's only that you are here and you saw. And you heard it all.' She shook a finger at him. 'And I think you saw him go in there. Didn't you?'

'Yes,' he said meekly.

She threw up her hands. 'Say what you want to whoever you want. It doesn't matter. The whole block knows now. This is a gossip factory. Everybody knows everything.' She leant in close. 'Did you know Kennedy was Sol's father?'

'No, I didn't.'

'Why do you think Kennedy didn't drive them out?'

That made sense. And then a thought.

'Why not your family?' he said.

She wiped an eye with a finger. 'Because he liked my girls.'

Chapter 34

Jack worked on. There was no sign or message from Ben and Tony. He was reconciled to working alone. Ben presumably was sorting out Tony or the stairs or both. Jack could phone him and find out, but he'd only be told to carry on. What other instruction could there be?

Kennedy was Sol's father. Well, well. Mitzi the mother was working for him. Nothing new, employing the wife, except he doubted they were ever married. How old was Mitzi? If she was about Heidi's age, then she must have been a young teenager when Sol was born. That figured, knowing Kennedy's preferences.

Sol was working for him too, laundering money. A real family business, with dad firmly in control. Who would gain by his death? That was the question, favoured by TV cops. Mitzi would be free of him, but she'd run off ahead of his death. Heidi was free too, but on the way to becoming homeless, though she'd picked up his stash. Sol was out of a job. And his pa wouldn't have left a will. So who would his estate go to? Sol could have been banking for him, might have a good idea how much he'd stashed away. Could Sol get the lot when things were finally sorted out? That depended on how many other kids Kennedy had scattered around. Or whether the cops decided it was proceeds of crime and collared the lot.

A crunching from the garden door caused him to turn. The elderly black man with the basket on wheels was coming though, his basket no doubt stuffed with sin and doom, more than enough to match Pandora.

He stopped by Jack.

'Have you been sentenced to hard labour, young man?' he said with a grin.

'I've done some things in my time,' said Jack. 'This is my punishment.'

'And have you confessed to God?'

'No.'

'Why not? Are you too lazy, too proud? Or mired in disbelief?'

'All three, I should think,' said Jack.

The man shook his head. 'Time is short, young man. The end time is upon us. What will you say when you are before the Angel of the Lord?'

Jack considered this prospect. His judgement.

'I'd tell him, I was a builder who tried to do a decent day's work. Didn't get rich, so that must give me a better chance of getting through the eye of a needle than a rich camel. There'll be lots worse than me in line. What about you, demanding we all get saved? What will you say to the Angel at the Gates?'

The old man smiled. 'You are astute, young man. You have hit the big one. Shall I be saved? I have dwelt on that for many years, and can only hope, in the final judgement, that I have done enough. When I was young, I was evil. I make no bones about it, utterly evil. Not a word I use lightly.'

Jack had his doubts, but held his tongue.

'My youth was iniquity upon iniquity. I had women by the score, treated them badly. I took drugs, sold drugs. I drank enough alcohol to sink a battleship. I stole anything that wasn't tied down. I was always in brawls. If a man looked at me sideways, I would strike him. That's how wicked I was. A mere look!'

He was gripping the handle of his basket on wheels as if it might run off without him.

'When I was 25 I nearly killed a man. A fight in Stratford. You know the Two Puddings?'

'Bit of a dive,' said Jack. 'I went there a few times. Drugs and fights.'

'And half naked girls. Exactly my scene. A man said something cheeky to a girl I had picked up. So naturally, I hammered him until he was senseless. The police picked me up. I admitted that it was me. There were too many witnesses to argue. In jail, sobering up, I had my epiphany. And I prayed the man would live. And the Lord answered. I see the man sometimes, fifty years on. He limps still. My rheumatism is my punishment.'

He laughed indicating his knees.

'I was three years in prison. I have no complaints. I got off lightly. In my time I had more knives than a cutlery drawer. Guns, razors. I robbed small shops. I beat my father black and blue.' He held Jack's eye. 'I know about sin.'

'You were a mean geezer.'

'When I was drunk or out of my head on drugs, no man or woman was safe from me. When I was sober I was hardly better. I scattered my seed as if to populate the globe after the flood. I was a villain, until that day in the prison cell when I was reborn.'

He stopped and waved a finger, which might be an admonishment for Jack or himself.

'Well you may ask me, young fellow, have I done enough. All I can say to you is, I do not know. My destiny lies no longer in my hands, but with our Father in Heaven. I go to church, I worship daily. Several evenings a week, with others from the congregation, I take food and drink to the homeless. I pray with them. But is that enough?'

'You must have made up for your youth by now,' said Jack. 'How does it go? *More joy shall be in heaven over one sinner that repenteth...*'

'*Than over ninety nine just persons.* St Luke 15:7. Well remembered, young man. But that does not concern evil, real evil. Suppose Hitler, in his shelter in the final days of the war, had begged on his knees for forgiveness for murdering six million Jews and starting a war? Would he be forgiven? I asked my pastor and he said, yes, God would forgive even him. But I don't believe it. Some sins are beyond salvation.'

'And yours?'

'I don't know.'

'I am sure you are forgiven,' said Jack, wondering though whether the man wanted it both ways. To be the biggest sinner in order to be the grand seller of salvation. A lot he knew.

He said, 'You must live at number 5, top floor.'

'Yes, I do. That bit nearer Heaven.'

'What do you know about flat 6?'

'No one is living there, but I hear noises sometimes. Well, I haven't for a few days. But there were lights on. I saw Kennedy go in and out, sometimes with a young girl or two. I think they were making pornography. As if the world hasn't enough dirty pictures. That devil's spawn, Kennedy, he drove out Mr Ballard and his wife. They had loud parties so I was glad when they went, but I feared Kennedy would move in his whores. But he didn't. Just the odd girl from time to time for his porn. I tell you, he is now in Hell, burning in the fiercest fire. Of that you can be sure.'

'Mr Ballard might return?'

'I hope not. But I will survive his rhythm and blues. And I must leave you. I have shopping to do and church business.

Gossip paves the way of the sinner. Look to your salvation, young man. Time is short.'

And he left Jack to contemplate the state of his soul.

He worked on for another hour and decided that he was done for the day. It was nearly four o'clock, he had been abandoned, and he'd had enough of dust and grime.

Chapter 35

As he climbed the stairs to his flat, Jack could hear sounds inside. If it was Tony back for another going over, he'd break every bone in his body. He crept stealthily up.

Music was playing. Violin, jazzy guitar. He knew who it must be.

He opened the door to see Mia putting socks and underwear back in a drawer. She was in school uniform, light blue blouse and navy trousers. Her bulging bag lay on the sofa.

'You're filthy,' she exclaimed. 'What have you done to your head? What's happened to this place?'

She turned off the music.

'Was that Stéphane Grappelli?'

'Yes, with Django Reinhardt at the Hot Club de France. Don't change the subject. What's happened to you?'

No way round it. The state of the flat and his head deserved explanation. Jack told her how he got the blow on the head, without telling her about Tony and Heidi. And finding he'd been burgled when he got back from hospital.

'You're not safe to be let out,' she said. 'Go and have a shower. You're filthy. I'll see what we've got in the first aid box and redo your dressing.'

She was firm like her mother. Though he didn't object to her commands. It saved further detail on the injury and aftermath. Besides which, he was dirty with all the grime of the hallway. In the bathroom, he had trouble finding clean clothes and took a shirt out of the dirty washing. It was grubby but not as much as the one he'd taken off.

He showered and soaped and let the hot water wash away his sin. Always a good place to think, the shower. Though a bath was more of a soothing wallow, but with a dirty job the bath water would be filthy, and cling to him as he climbed out. A shower washed it away, and there was no bath to clean. Or leave dirty.

Jack hoped Ben would be back tomorrow. Though if the choice was Ben and Tony, he'd rather work on his own, thank you very much. It had to be admitted the three of them could clear the rubble in an hour or two. Not that he'd done much today, two hours max.

Blame Tony.

Flat 6 on the top floor niggled at him. The cops must have been up there, surely? Certainly, they must have questioned all the residents of Cromer Court. But the empty flat at the top, had they been in?

Jack dressed and tore off the dressing on his head, wincing as it took hair with it. It wasn't that cruddy as it had been under his helmet when working. Still, grubby enough.

When Jack came out of the bathroom, there was Mia with the first aid box. Alison had bought it for them, saying every house should have one. You never knew what might happen. Not a saying he could argue with, having been hit from behind on a footbridge.

'You've got six stitches,' said Mia. She had sat him in a chair and was standing over him. The first aid box and scissors were on the table.

'They dissolve in a few weeks,' he said.

She rubbed in antiseptic firmly. A little too firmly, and he winced. She admonished him, saying the wound had to be clean. Mia wiped off the excess with cotton wool and laid over the wound, lint and strips of plaster. He had the feeling he looked like a dog's dinner, or was that just vanity?

His daughter stood back to look him over. 'A bit lumpy, but you're covered up. And I must go. I only dropped in to tell you about the cello. I forgot all about it, as I've been tidying up, though you wouldn't think so to see this place. And then listening to you going on about being bashed on the head.'

'What's happening about the cello?' he said, feeling the dressing. Yes, it was lumpy. But, as she said, it covered.

'I had to give it back,' she said. 'Mum phoned school, but it did no good. No exams, no cello. That's the rule. I can't make exceptions, said Mrs Tulloh. She's the music teacher. There's other girls want it, and so on and so on.' She stopped. 'In short, I am no longer a cellist.'

'We could get you one,' he said too quickly. Not wise, but it's what a good parent might say.

'Got a spare 500 quid?'

'No.'

'That's no surprise. Mum has, but I know her strategy. She'd make me promise this, that and the other. And then just wait me out, until I've forgotten all about the cello.'

'I'll think about it,' he said, sufficiently non-committal to mean anything or nothing. Most likely the latter.

'You do that. Have a look on eBay for prices. But I won't be signing up for any concerts.'

A few minutes later, she left. He might look at eBay later, but suspected it would be a dismal search. And he had something more pressing to do. Even more than tidying the flat.

He rang Fayyad.

Chapter 36

Twenty minutes later, he was outside Cromer Court in his van. He was wearing a woolly hat to cover the dressing, not wanting to have to say anything to Fayyad about the assault and burglary. He alighted and locked up, and sat on the low wall to wait. Someone had put a sofa in their skip, and what with the rubble, almost filled it. Ben's problem. There were compensations in not being in charge of a job.

It wasn't yet six o'clock, and would be light for more than three hours. It was warm, the sky almost clear, with a few wispy clouds here and here. But midsummer was not good for stargazing. The sun set too late; it wasn't worth going out till past 11 when the sun was well below the horizon. To think he had invited Heidi out with his telescope tonight on the Flats. You had to laugh. She'd accepted when she was a nurse, cancelled when she was Miss Whiplash.

Why was he still thinking of her? She preferred women anyway. Didn't like sex. Did weird things with lassos. He thought of cowboys pulling down steers. Who would be the steer in this case?

Did she wear spurs in bed? You'd end up with torn sheets, or maybe torn flesh. But who was to say what her punters wanted?

Fayyad arrived in his car. He parked and beckoned Jack over. Fayyad opened the car door and Jack climbed into the front seat next to his friend. Fayyad was wearing a light grey suit and, in spite of the warm weather, his tie was secure at the neck. Such details mattered to the man.

'I've got the keys,' he said. 'Kennedy kept a key-box. All keys labelled. This pair for flat 6.' He jangled the keys with their tag. 'What are you expecting to find?'

'I don't want to say.'

'Why not?'

'I don't want to look stupid.'

Fayyad laughed. 'At least we're not here mob handed at six in the morning. I've been there, Jack, believe me. We broke into this house. Police! Police! Armed response. And find a terrified young woman and three little kids. We search every room, guns first. Nothing. Crap intel. The front door smashed in. More than a dozen of us, front and back. Cost a fortune. There's stupidity for you. And as far as I know no one got a reprimand. Buried in paperwork somehow.' He stopped, smiled. 'This one is simple. Just you and me, mate. Cost as far as the office is concerned, zero. So what are you expecting?'

'Kennedy used the flat for making porn films. No one lives there. I just have a feeling... Can we leave it there and go and look?'

'The boss would shoot me for allowing such evasions. Though we should have gone in anyway. I don't know how it got omitted. But OK, I won't push you further. Empty flat or bone-yard, let's find out.'

They left the vehicle. And went up the path, which Jack had traipsed too many times, back and forth with the wheel-barrow.

In the hallway, they edged past the mound of rubble.

'Crime scene have left flat 1,' said Fayyad, indicating the door.

'I met Amir today,' said Jack. 'The actual tenant. Wants me to decorate, but he has to get the flat cleared.'

'It's pretty full, I can tell you. He liked African artefacts. Masks and shields, spears, that sort of stuff. Must be worth quite a bit.'

They went out the back door and into the garden, a rectangle of grass, the lawn needing a cut, with a few isolated shrubs along the fence on either side. Jack and Fayyad climbed the fire escape, which had a door at each landing. They went up slowly, to keep down the sound of their footsteps on the metal steps.

'What more have you found out about Kennedy?' asked Jack as they reached the first landing.

'Kennedy Gerrard is not his real name. We have his fingerprints on record. He was jailed for paedophilia and released about ten years ago. And disappeared off radar. He should have been regularly reporting to the police. But he did a runner. I don't know how many aliases he's had since.'

'Self employed,' said Jack.

'You might say,' said Fayyad. 'Paying no tax, so strictly off the system. Until he gets murdered.'

They had gone in the door of the first floor. They would go up the other two floors inside the building. They halted, engrossed in conversation.

'But here's a thing,' said Fayyad, speaking in a hushed voice. 'First DNA results are back. And it turns out Mitzi... You know Mitzi Baldwin?'

'Sol's mother. Went off with a Nigerian, they say. Lived in one of these two flats on this floor.'

'That one, flat 3.' He pointed it out. 'Well, Mitzi, it turns out, is Kennedy's sister.'

'You are joking.'

'I was surprised too. So I phoned and checked they'd got it right. Confirmed. They share 50% of their DNA. So brother and sister.'

They had begun climbing the inside stairs up to the top floor.

'Have you the results of Sol's DNA?' said Jack.

'Not yet. It's in progress. Why?'

Jack smiled. He was ahead of the law in his collection of gossip.

'He's Kennedy's son,' he said.

'Well, well,' said Fayyad. 'Brother and sister having a child. Why does that barely shock me? When I first started this job, I was in disbelief much of the time. What people did to each other. I was gobsmacked, day after day.' He shrugged. 'Now? Incest is routine. I wonder what's happening to me.'

'How old was Mitzi when she had Sol?'

'Let me work it out. 33 now, Sol's 19. She was 14 when she gave birth, so 13 when she conceived. A rape victim, I'm sure.'

'How old was Kennedy?' said Jack.

'36 now, the corpse anyway. 19 years ago, he'd have been a 17 year old father.'

'And uncle.'

'Let's go in before you befuddle me further.'

They went to the door of flat 6. No lights showed from the window above the door. Fayyad put his ear to the door; there was no sound from inside. There were two locks. Fayyad opened the top with one of the two keys, then the lower. He pushed the door open.

Chapter 37

There were several rooms in the flat, and little furniture. In the kitchen, there was a sink, a few plates and cups in a rack on the draining board, a microwave on a corner shelf. There was a single plastic chair by a bin full of empty foil containers.

And a familiar smell. A scent Jack knew.

The bathroom had a toilet, a shower in the bath with curtains on the rail. There was liquid soap on the sink ledge and a large grubby white towel over the radiator.

The same smell.

The largest room, which would have been the sitting room in an occupied flat, was empty, apart from two plastic chairs. No carpet on the floorboards. Jack and Fayyad moved on. There was a small bedroom which had a clothing rail of stripper type costumes on hangers or laid on top: frilly bras and knickers, wispy boas, fishnet stockings, suspender belts, and on the floor beneath, a range of high heeled shoes and calf length boots. In a corner was a tea chest spilling over with whips, handcuffs, masks, wigs, canes of various thickness and length, chains and rope.

'The costume and props department, I assume,' said Fayyad.

'And that must be the studio,' said Jack, indicating the room they hadn't been into, the door closed.

He noted the hefty door. Sound proofing. You'd want that for a studio. Jack opened the door, and was struck by the stench that came out of the darkness. Urine, faeces, stale air and sweat. What on earth went on in here? In the gloom, Jack had trouble finding the switch.

'Stinks like a bunged up toilet,' exclaimed Fayyad. He'd taken out a handkerchief and put it to his nose and mouth.

As his hand searched the wall, Jack said, 'Soundproof board on the walls. The door fitting is snug. Some money has been spent here.'

He found a dimmer switch and twisted it on full.

The flood of light revealed a woman in bra and panties on the floor, tied up at her feet and ankles in yellow rope.

Dead or unconscious?

'Stay at the door, Jack,' ordered Fayyad.

He went to the woman, knelt down and put a hand to her mouth. Unsure, he felt the artery in her neck. The woman was black, her Afro hair messy and tangled. She lay crumpled, on her side, bound legs pulled to her stomach, chest almost meeting them, foetal position.

'She's alive,' said Fayyad.

'How long has she been here?' said Jack, at the door.

'Kennedy must have left her. He's been dead four days. So at least that.'

'Looks like a set for a snuff movie,' said Jack, taking in the rest of the room.

There was a sofa at the back. Long blackout curtains were on the window behind. A side window was similarly covered. Against a wall were photographic lights and a fancy camera on a tripod. In the centre was a low butcher's block, scored and blood stained. On it, a cleaver and several long knives.

The block and contents held him. He gasped at the thought of what might have gone on here, if Kennedy hadn't been halted.

'Mitzi, is it?' he said.

'Yes,' said Fayyad. He was now wearing latex gloves and had taken one of the knives from the block to start sawing at the rope on her hands. 'I've seen pictures of her, though looking much better than this. Phone the ambulance, Jack. I'm calling the station. This is a crime scene.'

Jack dialled 999.

'And once you've done that,' went on Fayyad, 'you must leave. The less contamination of the scene the better.'

Jack had the phone to his ear. The response came quickly.

'Emergency Services. What service do you require?'

'We need an ambulance,' said Jack. 'There's an unconscious woman at 6 Cromer Court, Forest Gate. Please come as soon as you can. The police are already here.'

Chapter 38

On the phone, Jack told the emergency service operator that the paramedics would need to go through the hallway and then upstairs via the fire escape in the garden to the top floor. The operator asked about Mitzi's condition. He told them as much as he knew, that she'd been abandoned for four days or more without food or water, tied up, and that a policeman was with her. And that he had to leave as it was now a crime scene.

He closed the call and heard Fayyad talking to a colleague on his phone, explaining where he was and what he was seeing. Mitzi was lying on her back, Fayyad had cut off the bonds. Jack could just see the faint rise and fall of her chest. Bits of rope and faeces were scattered around her. He knew better than to ask Fayyad to tidy up. This was evidence. Even the faeces told a tale.

'Shall I get her some water?' he said.

'Leave it,' said Fayyad. He had closed his phone call. 'She's unconscious. And ten minutes won't make any difference. We don't want to suffocate her. Let the professionals handle it.'

Jack could see the sense of it. Stupid to kill someone who had hopefully been saved. He wondered how much longer she might have survived. You can live weeks without food, but only days without water.

He left the flat. In the hall, he breathed deeply, free of the stench of the room. Poor Mitzi, tied up and lying in her own shit in full view of the butcher's block. She wouldn't have known Kennedy was dead. So she'd be thinking that he could be back for her anytime. With the soundproofing, no one could hear her as she screamed.

And all the time, with her up here trussed, he had been working downstairs. Life had been going on in the block. The cops came and went, as did the residents, while upstairs in flat 6 Mitzi was abandoned.

Heidi's perfume. Definitely. In the kitchen, in the bathroom. She had been up here. And the yellow rope round Mitzi's ankles and wrists, the same as the lasso. Had she been in it with Kennedy?

And then the thought, the horror, that she had known all the time. She had left Mitzi to die.

He clambered down the fire escape, legs weak and hollow. He could hear a siren, must be the ambulance on the way. They hadn't wasted time. The police needn't rush; there were no criminals to catch in the act. And Fayyad was there anyway.

At the ground floor, Jack went through the garden door, past the rubble and two downstairs flats. And on, down the path to the street.

He waited. After perhaps a minute, the ambulance pulled up, the siren ear-piercing close up. It was shut off and a woman and a man in green uniform jumped out of the vehicle.

'Upstairs, flat 6,' exclaimed Jack. 'I'll show you. You'll need a stretcher.'

'Thanks,' said the woman. 'Let's get the gear,' she said to her companion.

They opened the back of the vehicle. The man brought out a large box with a handle, the woman the stretcher.

'Show us the way,' said the man.

Jack directed them through the hallway and out into the garden.

'Top floor, flat 6. Up there,' said Jack, pointing up the fire escape. 'The flat door is open.'

'Thanks, mate,' said the woman.

And the two went up the fire escape. Jack watched them climb up the two levels to the top floor and go in the landing door. There was nothing he could do here. The police would be here soon enough. He was superfluous.

As he was going through the hallway, Heidi's door opened.

'What on earth is going on?' she said. 'All that noise. Sirens.'

She was in a long dressing gown, barefoot. And the scent, the very same.

'They've found Mitzi,' he said.

'Where?'

He looked her hard in the eye. 'You know where.'

'What are you saying, Jack?'

'Cops'll be here in a minute.' He looked down the hallway to the street door as if they might be imminent. 'Do you want to speak out here or inside?'

She considered for a second.

'Come in.'

He followed her down her hallway to the kitchen. She had tidied away the lasso. The same rope that had bound Mitzi. The same scent pervading the flat.

'Tea?' she said.

He almost laughed at the incongruity; a woman upstairs almost dead, and Heidi offering tea.

'Yes,' he said.

She put on the kettle, and took down a biscuit tin which she put in the middle of the table. So nonchalant. As if she had no part in the goings on upstairs.

'How is she?' she said.

She had joined him at the table, taking a stool across from him. Her make-up was smeared. Did it always happen after a client?

'Alive,' he said, 'but not conscious. The paramedics have just gone up.'

'To where?'

'You know where.'

'That's the second time you've said that.'

She rose to get the teapot ready.

'Your scent is all around,' he said, 'and the same yellow rope as your lasso.'

'Ah.'

She dropped teabags in the pot as the kettle was whooshing to its end. She remained standing, biting a knuckle, watching him, as intently as he was watching her, each trying to catch in expression and body language what wasn't being said.

'You have reached a verdict,' she said. 'And found me guilty.'

His mind was racing. The scent upstairs was recent. Not four days old. She had been up between clients. Why?

As she poured tea in the pot, the oddities rebounded against the walls of his mind. She had been up after Kennedy was dead, while Mitzi was tied up in the studio. To do what?

'Why did you go up to flat 6?' he said.

'I made a couple of porn movies with Kennedy.'

'No, no. I don't mean ages ago. I mean the last few days,' he said. 'Since he's been dead.'

'I haven't been up there.'

'You're lying. Your scent is recent. You told me you are too used to it. You don't smell it any more.'

'You're a good listener,' she said with a tight lipped smile.

195

'I think you've been up there today. And you know what's there.'

'Do I?'

'You must do. It's a small flat, nothing much there. You didn't go up to use the microwave.'

'I have one here, without going to the top floor to heat a pie.'

'It's a fit up,' he said.

'What do you mean?'

'I mean...' he was thinking quickly, trying to place the pieces so they made a coherent picture, 'I mean you and Mitzi are in it together.'

'In what?' she said as she poured tea into the cups.

Jack watched Heidi as she put down the pot, and poured milk into both cups, with a shaky hand she struggled to control. Heidi knew that he knew.

'Mitzi killed Kennedy,' he said.

She laughed. 'That's ridiculous, Jack.'

'It's the only way it makes sense,' he said. 'Why would you go up to flat 6? Kennedy is dead. Upstairs is Mitzi, who shared your working life, bound hand and foot.'

'If I had seen her like that, I would have untied her.'

'I am sure you did. Every so often, when you could, you popped up, untied her, fed her, and bound her again.'

'Why would I go through such a stupid rigmarole?'

'Because she killed Kennedy. Her alibi is that she couldn't have done it as she was tied up on the top floor in readiness for a snuff movie. You and she concocted it.'

Heidi pushed him over a mug of tea. She opened the biscuit tin. And stretched over to the draining board for two small plates.

She was shivering. This had to be the right lines. She was afraid of him.

'Mitzi went off to the casino with her Nigerian. That was a week ago,' he said. 'But she didn't go to Nigeria.'

'Where did she go?'

'That's a puzzle,' he said. 'Obviously she might have gone anywhere, but Kennedy kept her short of cash, so she had limited options. But she had a plan, and needed to be here. She couldn't stay here with you; Kennedy would find her. She couldn't go to her flat with Sol. He'd find her there too. Mrs Nawaz wouldn't take her in, she has enough problems with her husband. So that leaves the West Indian man, the bible basher. I don't know his name.'

'Mr Thomas. He's from St Kitts.'

'It seems unlikely,' he mused. 'But then again, a fallen woman would be quite a coup. He'd certainly want to save her soul. That would give him extra points for the last judgement. Probably he didn't know her further plans. Did you know Mitzi was Kennedy's sister?'

'As a matter of fact, I did. Have some shortbread. They're genuine Scottish, made with butter.'

'I'll stick with tea, thank you.' He took a sip as if to emphasise his intention. 'Kennedy, her brother, raped her when she was a teenager. Probably many times. Then their lives go in separate directions. She hopes she's seen the last of him. But then he comes back into her life, pimping her. Keeping her on the tightest rein.'

'She hated him,' said Heidi. 'He was a rat. Imagine being a kid, living in the same house as Kennedy. Repeated abuse. Everyone has their limit.'

Both had gone quiet, taking in Mitzi's past with her present: the body of her brother in flat 1, and she bound on the top floor.

'There was the fire in the hallway,' said Jack, 'about the time she pretended to leave with the Nigerian. I thought the fire was coincidence. Kids smoking weed in the hallway.'

197

'And now you don't.'

'You and Mitzi needed keys. For his flat and for flat 6. With the fire, he has to leave. He's stoned most evenings. So you help him get out. He wants his flat locked after him, would do, considering what he's got there. So you oblige and get the keys from the key box. And at the same time, filch a spare set for Kennedy's flat and a set to flat 6.'

'Who do you think started the fire?'

'I'd guess it was you. You wanted the keys, so...' He stopped, reflected. 'Or could be Sol.' He bit his lip. 'I'll go for Sol.'

'Why would I bring Sol into it?'

'Easier for Sol,' he said weighing it up. 'Maybe you didn't want him involved, but I suspect his mother brought him in. Sol had no love for his father-cum-uncle, even though he did errands for him. Sol hated the way Kennedy treated his mother. I think he was promised the cash in the flat. I saw him putting it in a machine at AttaBet. Laundering it, setting himself up for a life of crime. Sol started the fire, let it burn awhile, then called the fire brigade. No loss of life, jobs for the builders, and you got the keys.'

'You have a vivid imagination,' she said. 'It must be the cold nights out with the telescope.'

'It connects,' he said. 'Mitzi came down from Mr Thomas' flat one night, when Kennedy was stoned. Killed him. And then she went upstairs to flat 6 with you. Showered thoroughly. You tied her up, and took away her blood splattered clothes, dumped them somewhere, miles away. Her alibi was perfect: Kennedy was holding her to make a snuff movie.'

'More tea?'

'Please.'

She poured him another cup and some for herself. She took a shortbread biscuit, munching it slowly.

'Someone reported Kennedy's murder,' Jack continued. 'I can't say who. You or Sol most likely. The cops come, break in, and find Kennedy's body. All part of the plan. They questioned the residents. Expected. But they didn't go into flat 6. How frustrating that must have been for you. Poor Mitzi bound in that smelly room. Leaving her with her faeces was a good touch. Well, for a short stay, increasingly unpleasant as time went by. And you went up periodically between clients to release the bonds, feed her, retie her. What a chore!'

'It was,' she said.

'You couldn't even report it. Even anonymously. Or the cops would know someone else was involved. The cops had to find it for themselves. But they didn't connect the flat on the top floor with the murder at the bottom.'

Neither spoke for a minute. Jack drank his tea. She dipped the remnant of her biscuit into hers. And watched it soften, break up and fall into the liquid.

'What do you suggest I do?' she said.

'Pretty obvious what to do,' he said.

'Kill you?'

'I don't think that's your style. Mitzi is the killer, not you.' He drank some tea. He watched the woman watching him. And wondered what she would offer him. Money or sex?

'I made the connections,' he said. 'But then I've been around the place and got to know everyone. The cops might well catch up.'

'How much do you want?'

Jack shook his head. 'Too risky. I'm not going inside for a few thousand.'

'Are you going to turn me in?'

'No.'

'Why not?'

'Kennedy was a rat. Mitzi was raped by him and controlled by him. He drove people out of their homes, had underage sex, sold drugs to anybody and everybody. I'm sure there's a few crimes I've omitted, but that's a good enough list. I'll leave the cops to do their work.'

'Thank you,' she said. 'I'll get rid of the lasso. Silly keeping it. And that scent. I just don't smell it any more.'

'If you've got any air freshener, spray every corner of this place.'

She stood up.

'The cops will be here shortly,' she said. 'So I think you'd better leave. Thank you for the chat. But I've things to do.'

Chapter 39

Back home, Jack tidied up for a while. Mia had done some clearing up, and been more thorough than he was being. Folding clothing, while he just bundled items away. He knew that if he were doing it for someone else, after a job say, he'd be neater. But then he'd be getting paid for it, and would be judged for it.

Here, he had no judge. Not totally true. Mia popped over on her way back from school, stayed every other weekend and odd days when her mother was busy. Alison came from time to time. The harshest judge, and no bad thing, having witnessed Ben and Tony's squalor.

It was boring, tidying up. A job that needed doing over and over. Ben and Tony's solution was to opt out of it. Well, you couldn't absolutely, but you could leave it until the sink was full, forcing on you the necessity to wash a cup. Everything tended towards untidiness. The law of the universe, he'd been thinking about it the other day. Back it comes. We fight it all our lives, some more than others, and die, leaving others to tidy our remnants.

It was his job as a builder to fight the untidiness. Put slates back, renew wood and windows, re-hang doors, point brickwork, rebuild fallen walls, plaster and paper over the cracks. But the cracks would always win. Ice caps broke off, chalk cliffs fell into the sea. Everything crumbled to dust.

Doom-laden stuff. He turned on the TV, but couldn't laugh along with the family in the show. Their banter, their sexual meandering. It was all made up. While in Cromer Court there was murder, incest, cover up. Heidi in costume, play acting, though how convincing would you have to be for a pumped up punter? Whips, lassos, and high heeled shoes. The props, the costumes, and a feeble script with a little improvisation every time.

Absurd. Mr Thomas from St Kitts had the answer. On your knees, pray to be saved. And then it made sense. Life and death hung together. Life was the trial, the examination. Kennedy had failed. Where did that leave Mitzi and Heidi?

He that is without sin amongst you, let him cast the first stone.

Echoes of Sunday school.

You'll never go to heaven in a bottle of gin
'Cos the Lord don't let no spirits in.

Where on earth did that come from? How deeply buried, that week at the scouts, a campfire in Epping Forest. Though the sentiments held. Gin was no way to get through the Pearly Gates. He had faith in that.

Fayyad phoned.

'How's it going?' said Jack.

'Crime scene are up in flat 6, going about their business. And I'm at the hospital.'

'How's Mitzi?'

'Better than expected. She's woken up. They've washed her. Put her in a hospital gown and she looks quite civilised. Even talking a little.' He stopped for an instant. 'Thing is, Jack, I'm wondering if it's all a bit speedy.'

'What do you mean?'

'I'm wondering whether it could have been fixed. We were meant to find her, all tied up in the flat.'

'I don't follow,' said Jack, though he most surely did.

'Perfect alibi,' Fayyad said. 'If she'd killed Kennedy.'

'She couldn't tie herself up,' said Jack.

'Sure, she'd need an accomplice. I was thinking of that other working girl, Heidi Miles.'

'Seems pretty complicated.'

'Things are not always simple, Jack. Criminals can be devious.'

'I'm sure you'd know. Have you got any evidence?'

'You sound just like my boss. Nope, just a hunch. It's a theory amongst others. Could be she was tied up by Kennedy and left there. Except she is recovering too quickly.'

'Tough girl perhaps.'

'Maybe. I need to be careful on this. There's a meeting in the morning, and I don't want to be the one laughed to the moon.'

'It's a theory amongst others,' said Jack. 'Go for the evidence.'

'You don't think it's far fetched?'

'What do I know? I'm a builder. Practical. Bricks, nails and timber. You've got to make it hold together, or it tumbles down on you.'

'Thought I'd sound you out. You saw the set up in flat 6, and you were right to go in. We should've looked earlier. Stay in touch.'

He rang off.

Jack went over the call as he made a cup of tea. Fayyad was going along the same track as he had gone. Although he himself had the advantage of being on the spot, talking to residents as they passed through the hallway. A short term advantage, as CSI crawled around flat 6.

Mitzi shouldn't have woken up so early, made so rapid a recovery. Thoughtless. She needed a relapse. And Heidi needed to look to herself.

Chapter 40

Jack didn't sleep well. Too much in his head to allow him to switch off. He'd got up about three in the morning and read a few pages in his book on the life of stars. But a few pages of stellar breakdown, the explosion of suns into supernovae, connected the deep space chaos to the chaos in his flat, his life, the mess in Cromer Court. How the laws of the big allied with the small.

He knew it was the danger of a little wisdom. With his scant knowledge, he was joining things up. He put mess at the centre as opposed to Mr Thomas who put Jesus Christ. Different ways of making a world.

His mother said, he thought too much. She sided with Mr Thomas. Though how do you stop yourself thinking? Drink, sex. The first was out, the second was occasional and certainly not lasting. Nothing was. He'd always be here, late at night, fighting with infinity.

He must do an evening class. Learn about art. Forget that, it was Alison's thing. Study insects, so many of them, birds, less of them, easier. How about trees? They were everywhere. And he barely knew one from the other. An oak had acorns. This road, Earlham Grove, had London planes on either side. And the rest of them? Trees.

But they were finite. Must be a tree course somewhere. Or maybe biology. Why had he wasted his school years? So much he knew nothing about. It overwhelmed him.

Jack managed a few hours' sleep. Enough so he could function. And daylight settled him. With a cup of tea, beans on toast, infinity floated off to the shore of unimportance, along with the flotsam and jetsam of his ignorance.

He was the first into work at Cromer Court. He wondered whether he'd be the only one today too. Whether Ben and Tony would deign to come in. Some job this was. The heap in the hallway barely looked smaller, then again, he hadn't done much yesterday. And it had just been him.

Jack began working, loading the wheelbarrow with the dust and rubble, finding space in the skip which now had the sofa precariously on top. If Ben had been here, they could have taken it off, but he was not going to do it on his own. He only had one back.

Heidi was coming down the road, swinging a hold-all. She was in jeans and a pink t-shirt, her hair frizzy. She wore trainers on her feet, which made him think how often he'd seen her barefoot about her flat.

She looked so light and pleasant. Pretty even without the cake of make-up. She was again the woman he'd first found attractive. He watched her coming, and sighed inwardly. If only she was a nurse.

A real one.

'Good morning, Jack,' said Heidi with a bright morning smile. 'I've been swimming at Atherton Leisure Centre. And I got rid of a few things on the way.'

'Like what?'

'You know.'

He surmised a lasso and a bottle of perfume.

'I've been washing clothing all night long,' she said. 'Perfume is so clingy. Look what I've bought.' She opened her hold-all. Inside was a rolled, wet towel and three canisters of air-freshener.

Jack examined one of the canisters.

'Forest Glade,' he read. 'Probably terrible for the ozone layer.'

'I don't give a monkey's about the ozone layer. I've that Asian cop coming in half an hour. I need to get in and get spraying. And put the last wash away.'

He was tempted to say that she might pay a visit to Mitzi in hospital and tell her to relapse. But he reckoned he'd been too helpful already. She was on her own. It was cops versus ladies of the night. He'd given assistance to both sides. That was him done with. It was down to Fayyad and forensics, and whether Mitzi and Heidi could hold their story together.

She left him, promising tea later.

Jack worked on, wheelbarrow after wheelbarrow, with each load attempting to find space between the sofa and the rubble already in there. The skip couldn't take much more.

He was at the skip, emptying a wheelbarrow when Fayyad and Hayley arrived. They gave him a wave and a call of Good Morning. He had no doubt Fayyad would have stopped for a chat if not with his colleague.

Not that Jack wanted to compare notes. He'd resigned. He was no longer a snitch. Do your own dirty work.

The two detectives went up the path, pressed one of the bells, although they could've gone straight in as the door was held open for Jack to go in and out. He was unable to hear the response, being too far back, but obviously they had one as they entered the hallway.

It was, as he'd suspected, a joint deputation for Heidi. She'd been swimming so she should be sharp. She would need to be. The door opened as the detectives arrived. He could just see her, she was holding a spray can. He hoped neither were allergic to Forest Glade.

Another quarter of an hour and Jack gave up. He couldn't get any more rubble in the skip. A new one was required, with or without the sofa, to get all the debris in. Were the stairs coming today? Ben and Tony Wilson weren't.

What on earth was going on with this job?

He phoned.

'Wilson and Son,' said Ben.

'This is Jack. I was on my own most of yesterday. No one here today. The skip is full. Where are the stairs? Where are you? What's going on?'

'You'd best come over, Jack. I've some things to say.'

'Like what?'

'Come over. I'll tell you then.'

Ben closed the call. Jack thought, not another delay on the job. Was Ben working another one, that Jack hadn't been told about? And doing both badly. It happened too often with small contractors. He'd done it himself, over committed, loath to lose the work. Moaned at by two parties.

Jack loaded his wheelbarrow and tools into the van. Leave nothing around, he'd learnt that too often. And drove off to Ben's. He wanted this sorted out. What was going on? It wasn't fair to leave him in the dark.

At the main road, he was snarled up in traffic. He pulled off, went round the houses, but got caught up in the school run, losing more than he had gained. Arriving at Ben's, he was further irritated by all the other vehicles on the road.

All with one driver in. How dare they!

He alighted and leaned against the van. Breathe slowly. Don't get into a row with the boss. That would never get anything achieved. He needed the work, he needed the money. Be helpful. Get an advance.

Jack rang the bell. And was surprised to see Ben open the door in a grey suit. He obviously wasn't planning to work today.

'Cup of tea, Jack?'

Having seen the state of the Wilsons' crockery, he politely declined.

'I've just had one,' he lied. 'The lady downstairs in flat 2 made me a cuppa.'

'Fine. Come into the sitting room.'

He followed Ben along the crowded hallway, the ladder and trestles pressing against them, and into the side room. The same, he recalled, on his visit with Mia. Stuffy, over-crowded, the desk piled with papers. Ben cleared a box of tiles from the sofa, looked around for a place to put them, and settled for under the keyboard.

Jack sat down. Ben sat on the keyboard chair. The other armchair was full of boxes, a languid saxophone blowing papers, and tiles galore.

'Tony not around?' asked Jack. Something to begin with, not that he cared.

Ben threw up a disparaging hand. 'He's in hospital.'

'How come?'

'Got into something he shouldn't have. A deal with dodgy gear. Got beaten up. They broke his jaw, three ribs busted.'

'Drugs, was it?'

'It was as it happens.' Ben looked at him closely. 'Do you know anything about it?'

'I heard some stuff went missing from Kennedy Gerrard's place.'

'Well, my smart son grabbed it. Figured he could play the big man. And got put in his place by a group of hoodlums.'

'I'm sorry about that.' He wasn't. Well, not for Tony, who had thumped him on the head and he still had the stitches, but he had sympathy for Ben.

'Never rains but it pours. I went to see him last night in hospital. He could hardly talk, his jaw had to be wired. He's got an operation today. I've got to go there in a few hours. The trouble he causes me.'

Jack hadn't come to talk about Tony's woes, though he didn't object to him being out of action.

He said, 'The job. The skip is full. When are the stairs coming? When are you coming in?'

Ben took a deep breath, and opened his hands plaintively. 'The thing is, Jack. I have to say this. No way round or through it. I am skint. Bankrupt.'

'What do you mean?'

'I mean the job is kaput. The bank has foreclosed. I am up to my neck in debt. I am well and truly busted.'

Jack was gasping, attempting to take it in. He should've guessed, all the signs were there.

'The job is done with,' he said slowly as Ben nodded. 'And my wages?'

Ben shrugged. 'You are one of the creditors. There's nothing I can do. I'm going to lose this house. The bailiffs are coming. They'll strip out anything of value. I'll be out on the street.'

'So I've been working for nothing. No payment?'

'Sorry, Jack.'

'Nothing at all?'

'As I said, you are on the list of creditors, but the tax people get the first snatch. Sorry, Jack. I know it's difficult, but see it from my end. I'm going to be out on the street. Twenty years I've lived in this house. And they get it. Every brick and slate.'

'You must've known this would happen when you took me on.'

'I hoped I could work my way out of it. You know how it is, the building game?' He was appealing builder to builder, his eyes wide, hands begging to be appeased. 'I thought with luck I could hold them off, do a deal, get more work in. I was owed two thousand quid by Barry Holden and he's gone bust. And that was the final straw. Down it all tumbled. Every door slammed in my face.'

'You owe me more than four hundred quid.'

'I owe others a lot more.'

'Have you gone bust before? Don't answer, you wouldn't admit it anyway.' Jack rose. 'There's no point me staying. I get the picture. A big fat zero.' A sudden thought. 'The bailiffs are coming to strip the house?'

'Tomorrow.'

'That saxophone. They don't know you got it.'

'Take it. I couldn't get along with it. Don't know why I bought it.'

Jack pulled it away from the boxes and papers.

'And how about the ladder in the hallway?' he said. 'Mine got nicked from my lock-up.'

'Take it. You're welcome to it. Much better you than the bailiffs. I'm sorry it's come to this.'

Jack was eager to get away from the apologies. Ben had half his sympathy, but he had his own trouble now as he wasn't going to get paid. As quickly as he could, he got out of the house with the ladder and saxophone. Ben didn't offer to help him, and Jack didn't mind.

What was there left to say?

He loaded the ladder onto the top of his van, tied securely with rope. He could always go window cleaning with a bucket and sponge. And that might not be a joke. The saxophone was on the seat beside him as he drove off.

No payment. That stung. Ben had gone bust. He needed work.

Jack thought of phoning his mate Bob. But it was Bob who had got him the job with Ben in the first place. So maybe not. And Tony was in hospital. Totally out of his depth with the drug deal. Heidi presumably didn't know her partner had bungled it. Then again, she had her own troubles with having to move flats and the law wanting answers.

She'd thrown away the rope in her flat, the perfume too. The cops might suspect she'd had a part in the murder, but they would have to prove it. Harder to do today than it would have been yesterday. He thought of her coming back from swimming, so light and attractive it had made his heart jump.

His head knew better. Sadly.

All the different people we are. He was a builder, a father, a lover infrequently, a son ditto, an astronomy freak. And an ignoramus, as Alison might remind him. He really must take a class this autumn, learn about culture. Science. It was so overwhelming.

Work, work. Concentrate. He must earn money.

He had a thousand or so work leaflets at home. Now he was jobless, he might as well post them door to door. Something to do when he got back to the flat. And text Mia about the sax. That would bring her over after school. Maybe she'd take to it, with the cello gone.

At least there'd be someone pleased to see him.

Thank you!

I am grateful to every reader who finishes one of my novels. I have taken you on a journey which I hope you have enjoyed. There are plenty of things you could have been doing, other than reading this book. So, thank you for your time.

If you liked *Jack in the Dust,* here's what you can do next:

I'd appreciate a review on Amazon. In that way, you can help me tell other readers about my books. Without reviews authors get few sales on Amazon. So I'd be grateful for your review to help this series get on the move.

You can get a FREE ebook of *Jack of Spades* or *Murder at Any Price* if you sign up for my readers' list. You may give it to a friend if you wish. When you sign up for my readers' list you will receive my regular newsletter. This will give you news about me, what I'm reading, and tell you about my future books, PLUS a variety of giveaways.

Sign up at my website:

DerekSmithWriter.com

Books by DH Smith

Jack Bell

These are all standalone novels and can be read in any order. They are:

Jack of All Trades

Jack of Spades

Jack o'Lantern

Jack By The Hedge

Jack In The Box

Jack On The Tower

Jack Recalled

Jack At Death's Door

Jack At The Gate

Jack In The Dust

Other Books

Murder at Any Price

Writing A Crime Novel

Books by Derek Smith

All my books, other than the Jack of All Trades series and *Murder at Any Price*, are written under the name Derek Smith.

Fantasy
Hell's Chimney
The Prince's Shadow

Other Books
Strikers of Hanbury Street (short stories)
Catching Up (poetry)

Young Adult Novels
Hard Cash
Half a Bike
Fast Food
Frances Fairweather Demon Striker!

Children's Novels
The Good Wolf
Feather Brains
Baker's Boy

For Younger Children
The Magical World of Lucy-Anne
Lucy-Anne's Changing Ways
Jack's Bus

About the Author

I live in Forest Gate in the East End of London. In my working life, I have been a plastics chemist, a gardener and a stage manager before becoming a professional writer. I began with plays, working with several theatre companies, and had a few plays on radio and TV, as well as on the stage.

In the early 80s I became involved in running a co-operative bookshop and vegetarian café in Stratford, where I learned to cook, and had my first go at writing a novel. The first was a mess, and, after too many rewrites, binned. The transition from drama to novels took me a couple of years to get to grips with.

My first success was a young adult novel, *Hard Cash*, published by Faber. Buoyed up by this, I stuck with children's work, did school visits, and made a hand to mouth living as a full time author, topped up with some evening class work in creative writing at City University and the Mary Ward Centre in Holborn. A few adult fiction titles appeared from time to time, between the children's list, and I have since been working more in that direction with my Jack of All Trades series.

DerekSmithWriter.com

The book you've been reading was designed by Lia at

Contact lia@freeyourwords.com for a quote

www.ingramcontent.com/pod-product-compliance
Lightning Source LLC
Chambersburg PA
CBHW061322200626
46813CB00017B/2816